DEATH BEFORE DISHONOR

NEW WORLD PICTURES
IN ASSOCIATION WITH
BALCOR FILM INVESTORS
present

A LAWRENCE KUBIK/M.P.I./BIMA *Production*

DEATH BEFORE DISHONOR *Starring* FRED DRYER BRIAN KEITH JOANNA PACULA

Director of Photography DON BURGESS *Screenplay by* JOHN GATLIFF & LAWRENCE KUBIK

Executive producers FRANK CAPRA, JR. ARTHUR MASLANSKY WILLIAM BRAUNSTEIN

Produced by LAWRENCE KUBIK *Directed by* TERRY LEONARD 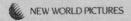 NEW WORLD PICTURES

 NEW WORLD PICTURES

A novel by Kevin D. Randle

Based on a screenplay by
John Gatliff & Lawrence Kubik

AVON
PUBLISHERS OF BARD, CAMELOT, DISCUS AND FLARE BOOKS

DEATH BEFORE DISHONOR is an original publication of Avon Books. This work has never before appeared in book form. This work is a novel. Any similarity to actual persons or events is purely coincidental.

AVON BOOKS
A division of
The Hearst Corporation
1790 Broadway
New York, New York 10019

Copyright © 1987 by New World Pictures, Ltd.
Published by arrangement with New World Pictures, Ltd.
Library of Congress Catalog Card Number: 86-91017
ISBN: 0-380-75282-4

First Avon Printing: January 1987

AVON TRADEMARK REG. U.S. PAT. OFF. AND IN OTHER COUNTRIES, MARCA REGISTRADA, HECHO EN U.S.A.

Printed in the U.S.A.

K–R   10   9   8   7   6   5   4   3   2   1

PROLOGUE

The roar of the twin General Electric T58-8 engines and the popping of the dual-rotor systems filled the cargo compartment of the helicopter, making speech impossible for all except the crewmen who wore helmets linked into the aircraft's communication network. Eight Marines sat in the darkened interior, staring at each other across the narrow deck, barely visible in the dim red lights, waiting. All were dressed in camouflaged fatigues, their faces hidden by green, brown, and black stripes of camo paint, and were wearing combat gear. Each held a rifle, the butt on the deck and the muzzle pointing upward. They were a silent, grim group who wouldn't have been talking even if they could have heard each other over the engine noise.

The Marine team leader had moved to the open hatch of the CH-46 helicopter and was staring into the blackness of the night. He was older than the others, taller than any of them, bigger. His uniform fit him closely, looking like it had been tailored to him. In addition to the combat gear, he wore a pistol on his hip and had a large Kabar taped upside down to the shoulder straps of his harness.

Outside he could see little other than the silver of

1

the ocean below and the blaze of stars overhead. He watched the waves slip under the aircraft for a moment, and then turned and stared at the tiny light set near the door that was glowing bright red. He held a thumb up and four of the Marines stood up unhesitatingly. They lined up near the hatch.

The first was a young black man just a year out of high school. He was tall and wiry. His hair was hidden by the soft cap he wore and his features were hidden behind the smear of camo paint on his face. He glanced nervously at the team leader and then out the hatch.

Behind him was a thickly muscled man who looked no older than the black. There were a few splotches of white skin showing near his blue eyes. He tugged at his ear and then grinned at the team leader.

Next was a man who was probably twenty or twenty-one. He had spent a year in college, learning little, but drinking much. He decided that he needed a break from the books and the Marines would provide a perfect opportunity. He was short and stocky with black hair hidden under his cap. He looked at the deck, not wanting to see the team leader or what was happening outside the aircraft.

Last in the line was the oldest man, who was nearly twenty-three. He had been in the Marines for nearly two years, as an aircraft mechanic. He had decided that being a Marine meant more than fixing an airplane, so he had transferred. He was a thin man with sunken cheeks whose pale skin burned quickly in the sun. He looked like he would have been happier in a library doing research rather than waiting to leap out of a helicopter.

The noise of the engines changed as the helicopter

slowed, descending. When it was twenty feet above the surface of the water, the young black Marine jumped, feet first, his legs straight and his body rigid. He disappeared from sight in a splash of dark water, bobbed back to the surface, and turned in time to see the other three of his stick hit the ocean behind him. Then, in rapid succession, the four Marines who had been on the other side of the deck leaped from the aircraft. Slowly, as a body, the eight Marines began to swim toward the distant beach. Their lazy breaststrokes moved them through the ocean swell until they could feel the sandy bottom beneath their feet. Using the water as cover, they moved up the beach until they were near the tide line. The black Marine looked right and left, hesitated, and then rose up so he could sprint across the sand to a low bluff that would shield him from any sentries farther inland.

One by one the Marines left the water, each finding shelter near the bluff. From there they continued their advance, moving away from the stone and dirt of the bluff, to a fairly steep slope where they could use the terrain for cover. Cautiously, moving one at a time, using the brush, the trees, the depressions in the ground, they worked their way toward a sand-bagged bunker that was only a dark, shadowy shape in the bright moonlight.

The Marines froze as their team leader moved forward silently, his eyes on the back of the single sentry: a man who carried a modern automatic weapon in his hands as if waiting for the enemy to appear; dressed in tiger-striped jungle fatigues, he stood out in the open ground and in the moonlight. The team leader worked his way closer to the sentry, taking each step carefully, rolling his foot from heel to toe so that he didn't snap a twig or rustle a dry leaf. He took each breath slowly, rhythmically, almost forcing himself to be calm. As he lowered himself to the ground, letting his fingertips brush the dirt, he kept his mind focused on his task, his senses searching the earth around him.

He stopped suddenly as the sentry tensed, his head swiveling as he searched the night. The team leader heard the noise, too, and his eyes roamed until he spotted a ground squirrel skittering toward its burrow. The sentry began moving again, walking along his post.

Patiently, the team leader waited. He watched the sentry finish one cycle and turn to come back. When the sentry turned again, only a few feet from the team leader, he leaped. The sentry was surprised by the sudden sound behind him and spun, but the team leader seized the front of his uniform, swung a hip into him, and threw him to the ground. Before the sentry could move, the team leader landed on his chest, crushing the air from his lungs, one hand over the sentry's mouth and nose, the other holding his Kabar. With a single lightninglike thrust, he jammed it into the dirt next to the sentry's face, whose eyes followed the motion, staring at the blade that seemed to glow supernaturally with a light of its own.

Suddenly the whole area blazed with light as the floodlights came on, silhouetting the Marines against the background, picking them out of their cover, and displaying them for all to see. The team leader, now easily identifiable to all who watched as Gunnery Sergeant Jack Burns, stood up, his knife still in the ground by the sentry's face.

"You're dead, Private James," he said. Burns was a large man. He was nearly six feet six inches tall, with the wide shoulders and the narrow waist of an athlete, and looked like he could have played football professionally. He had short-cropped black hair, a well-tanned complexion that marked hours of training in the sun, and dark eyes. He reached down and pulled James to his feet in a single, fluid motion and then gestured him to join the other Marines in the bleachers set back from the sandbagged revetment that masqueraded as a bunker. There were fifteen or twenty men sitting in the bleachers, each dressed in camouflaged fatigues, waiting for their turn at the practice.

Burns stooped and pulled his knife from the dirt and began to pace in front of the bleachers, wiping the blade on his sleeve to clean it. He glanced at the young Marines, the contempt etched on his face.

As James sat down, Dino Ruggieri leaned close and whispered, "You're dead, Private James." Ruggieri was another of the young Marines, not yet twenty, who had the rugged good looks of a welterweight boxer. He had a dark complexion that was hidden under the camouflage paint, black hair that hung straight, and dark brown eyes.

Burns apparently heard the comment. He stopped pacing, and spun, flicking the knife into the bleachers, where it buried itself into a tar-stained post only six inches from Ruggieri's face.

"You candy-asses think this is funny?" he demanded in a voice filled with rage.

Ruggieri hadn't moved since the knife was thrown. He was sitting stiffly, his eyes fixed on the blade. He raised one hand to rub the sweat from his forehead, wiping it on the front of his camouflaged fatigues.

"All right, Ruggieri," said Burns quietly, "bring the knife down here."

Ruggieri reached out with his right hand and tried to pull the knife from the post, but it wouldn't budge. Finally he turned, put both hands on the hilt and levered it out in an up-and-down, rocking motion. He climbed from the bleachers and handed the weapon back to Burns.

Burns accepted the knife and slipped it back into the scabbard. "All right, Ruggieri, why did he fail?" asked Burns.

"He was indecisive," ventured Ruggieri.

"Indecisive! Ruggieri, you're right," said Burns as if he was surprised that anyone would come up with the right answer. "But now I'll show you the easiest technique for taking out a sentry. Turn and face the bleachers." Burns put his hands on Ruggieri's shoulders and spun him. "Soon as you feel the slightest pain, clap your hands. I'll release the pressure."

Ruggieri was tense. He wasn't sure what was going to happen to him. He brought his hands up slowly, the palms only two or three inches apart.

"Little more air between the hands," commanded Burns.

"Hey, Ruggieri, do it like you're showin' some broad the size of your dong."

Ruggieri looked into the bleachers and saw Sergeant Ramirez grinning at him. Ramirez was a buck sergeant who was one of the training NCOs and who had been in charge of the bleacher brigade until Burns had "killed" the sentry and taken over.

While Ruggieri had his attention diverted, Burns attacked swiftly and savagely. He slammed his forearm up under Ruggieri's throat and locked his hands, Ruggieri caught in a viselike grip in Burns's elbow.

Ruggieri couldn't move, couldn't think. He tried to clap his hands, but all the power seemed to have fled his arms, his hands held open by an unseen force. The night seemed to draw down around him, his vision shrinking until it seemed that he was staring down a long, dimly lit tunnel. In seconds, that too was gone and Ruggieri slumped against Burns, unconscious.

"A Marine is never indecisive," Burns informed them coldly.

The Marines looked at one another, speechless. The fun, the thrill had suddenly been swept from them. They glanced around at Ruggieri, who was beginning to stir, and then back at Burns. Private James sat upright as if in shock, impressed.

"A Marine attacks! Remember, combat is death. Yours or the enemy's."

Half a world away, Karl Gavril, a half-German, half-Algerian, crouched in the bushes outside a large frame house. His eyes were locked on a guard who stood on the veranda, partially hidden by the ivy climbing a thin, wooden trellis. The guard was a tall, thin man, wearing a khaki uniform. He held an Israeli Galil assault rifle in his hands, but leaned back against the side of the house, relaxed. He turned abruptly as something moved in the bushes, revealing that he wasn't nearly as relaxed as he seemed. He grinned as a cat pranced into view.

From inside the villa, Gavril could hear people sitting down to dinner. The noise of their conversation, the clanging of serving dishes, and the clatter of silverware masked any sound that he made. When he had a clear shot at the guard on the veranda, Gavril raised the silenced pistol he held, aiming carefully. There was a quiet *pop*. The guard jerked once, the top of his head blowing off, his blood splattering the side of the house as he collapsed. He held his rifle in a death grip as he slid down until he was on the floor of the veranda, his blood pooling under him. Then the rifle slipped from his nerveless fingers, landing beside his body.

As soon as the shot was made, another assassin, dressed in dark clothing that blended with the shadows of the night, moved through the dark to a position near the guard there. The man was smoking a cigarette, his Galil against the wall. He turned toward the trees, surveying them slowly but without real interest. The assassin raised her weapon, aiming carefully, and pulled the trigger twice, rapidly. The firing was lost in the sounds of the grounds around the house.

The first shot hit the guard high in the chest, stunning him. One hand groped for his weapon, but his fingers knocked it aside. The second spun him and killed him, his face against the rough side of the house. He dropped to the ground.

The assassin, Maude Wynter, a tall, slender woman with short-cropped blond hair partially hidden by the black watch cap she wore, moved past the dead man, picked up his weapon, and ejected the chambered round. She hit the magazine release and pocketed it. She tossed the rifle toward a bush, and away from the guard. Then, slowly, she opened the back door and silently entered the kitchen. She waited there for a moment, listening to the family in the other room. At an angle, through the open door she could see a man in his mid-forties at the head of a table spread with a white cloth and loaded with food. A large bouquet of flowers sat in the middle, flanked by two candelabra.

Sitting on the sides of the table were a teenage boy and girl. Wynter was surprised by the blond hair of the girl. The last person at the table was a woman, sitting with her back to the kitchen. Wynter heard something and stepped back into the shadows.

"Tova, bring some more meat, please," said the man to someone whom Wynter hadn't seen.

An instant later a fifth person appeared in the doorway. She moved across the kitchen, toward a counter, and then looked up to see Wynter standing there hiding in the shadows. Wynter smiled at her, as if to reassure her, and before the maid could move or speak, Wynter fired, the grin spreading on her face. The impact of the bullet pushed the maid back against the counter. Wynter fired a second time, the bullet punching into the maid's stomach, knocking her to the floor. As she fell, her hand hit a tray, spilling it.

The man at the table put down his fork, looked at the doorway, and then turned to his son. "Go and see what Tova dropped."

"Why me?" the boy whined.

"Because you are the closest."

"I'm always the closest," grumbled the boy, pushing his chair back. As the rest of the family laughed, he got to his feet and moved to the kitchen. He was approaching the door, but froze when he saw the maid sprawled on the kitchen floor, unmoving. He thought there was a pool of blood near her but couldn't be sure. He took a single step forward and then he saw Wynter.

She motioned him back into the dining room with a gesture from her pistol, her eyes locked on his. She followed him into the light. She smiled again, not a pleasant smile, but a grin of evil as she fired, the bullets from her silenced weapon driving the boy deeper into the room. He hit the edge of the table, his face blank, and fell to the floor, dragging the tablecloth with him, his blood staining the carpeting.

As Wynter shot the boy, Gavril crashed through the terrace door. The man stood then, half turned, and raised a hand in protest, but didn't speak. Several bullets from Gavril's silenced pistol slammed into him, pushing him toward the window. He spun, put out a hand as if to break his fall, and then collapsed, shattering the glass. He pitched out, disappeared from sight, dead before he hit the lawn.

The older woman, at first stunned by the swiftness of the murders, suddenly leaped to her left to protect her daughter. Both were screaming hysterically. Gavril turned toward them slowly and opened fire. The first shot hit the older woman, pushing her aside, her blood staining her chest. Wynter fired a moment later, the first shot hitting the daughter in the stomach. She sat down, her hand wrapped around her abdomen, the blood flowing between her fingers. She looked up, screaming, and was shot again. She slumped back, falling against her mother, who reached out as she died.

There was a sudden silence in the villa, broken only by the loud ticking of a clock. Gavril moved to the window, jerked the curtain aside and looked down on the body of the man lying there. Wynter pumped more bullets into the bodies in the dining room to make sure that each victim was dead.

Then, together, they both fled the house, found the motorcycles that they had stashed for their escape, and kicked them to life. There was a roar from the engines, and the two assassins hit the street, turning to the north and disappearing before anyone knew what had happened in the house.

CHAPTER ONE

Privates James and Ruggieri were standing at rigid attention, their eyes locked straight ahead. They were wearing clean T-shirts that were nearly virginal in their snowy whiteness, freshly pressed tiger-striped fatigue pants, and jump boots that glowed like black mirrors. Standing directly in front of them was Gunnery Sergeant Jack Burns. He was dressed the same, except that his T-shirt was jet black, and pinned above the left breast was a set of polished gold jump wings that sparkled in the light from overhead.

Around them the other members of the recon team stood at parade rest, all dressed like Burns and all wearing the gold jump wings. Cans of beer stood in rows on a long table in front of the men. A single light burned over them, bathing the scene. Lost in the shadows of the Quonset hut were the racks holding parachutes, chute bags, and repair equipment. The riggers' tables had been rearranged so that the men were standing either directly behind one, or in front of it. Black blinds had been pulled over the windows to shut out the outside world.

"Brothers," said Burns quietly, almost solemnly, addressing the senior men, "let us share the elixir of life with these two initiates."

A growl erupted from the senior men. None of them moved as they roared their approval.

"Drink!" commanded Burns. He watched as the ten men reached out for beer and drank from their cans in a precision move that looked rehearsed.

Burns turned his attention to James and Ruggieri. "What is a Brother of the Gold Wing? He can jump high, he can jump low. He jumps in water, jungle, sand, and snow. He's Para-Frog and a Devil-Dog. He's a Recon Marine."

Again a growl erupted from the senior men.

Burns took a pair of gold wings from his pocket and removed the clutch backs, exposing the metal studs. He stared at them for a moment, shined them against his T-shirt, and then said, "You are about to become privileged members of an elite society."

Burns stepped close to James and put the wings against his chest, pressing them through the cloth of the T-shirt and into the flesh of James's chest. James grimaced at the pain but didn't move and didn't speak. He shifted his eyes so that he could watch Burns's hand.

"And each of us wishes to personally participate with you in this great honor."

Burns doubled his fist and slammed it against James's chest, hammering home the wings, the sharp studs penetrating his skin. Blood slowly spread across the white of James's T-shirt, staining it crimson above the left breast. One by one each of the ten senior men approached, pulled the wings free, and then slammed his fist against James, driving the wings into him again and again. Throughout the whole ritual, James didn't move or cry out. He stood stiffly, his jaws clamped tightly, wishing that the ordeal would end, but damned if he was going to cry out in pain. He wouldn't let them know how much it hurt.

Now Burns approached him again, carrying a steel pot. He handed the helmet to James and each of the senior men emptied a can of beer into it. James lifted the helmet to his lips, using both hands, and began swallowing the beer as quickly as he could.

"So drink, Bloodwinger!" chanted the senior Marines. "Drink, Bloodwinger! Drink!"

Burns moved to Ruggieri and pinned a set of the gold wings on his chest. He hesitated an instant, then slammed his fist into Ruggieri's chest. As the blood began to spread, another of the senior Marines stepped to him, pulled them free and drove them home with a fist.

On the other side of the world, two men, stripped to the waist and sweating heavily, were sparring. One of them was a giant brute of a man named Abu-Jihar, who was about thirty-five. He had shaggy black hair that hung in wet strings on his face. He had a dense, close-cropped black beard, and large hands that looked like they could hide a basketball. The other man was nearly fifteen years younger, husky, but nowhere near the size of the older man. He too had black hair and a dark complexion. His naked chest and body glowed in the bright sun with a light coat of perspiration. Around them stood two dozen others, cheering them on—telling the young man he could beat the bear, could beat him easily.

The younger man moved in then, punching with both hands, a combination of blows that Jihar blocked easily as he danced away. The young man

hesitated, and attacked again, first with his fists and
the sides of his hands, then with his feet. He tried to
clip Jihar on the jaw with his foot, but Jihar blocked
the blow and countered with a whirling, reverse kick
that landed in the middle of his opponent's chest.
The young man fell to the sand heavily and did not
move.

"Now show them what you have learned," said
Jihar, looking down at his opponent. He held out a
hand to jerk the young man to his feet.

Off to his right, Jihar heard the quiet click of a
camera shutter and turned to see Elli Bauman, a
handsome woman, about twenty-four. She had long
dark hair, almost oval dark eyes, and a complexion
to match. She wore a khaki bush jacket and short
khaki skirt. Tan socks covered her legs to the knee.
She carried one camera, sighting through it, and had
two more hung on thin straps around her neck. She
also carried a large bag from a shoulder strap that
held her spare film, filters, and extra lenses.

Jihar tore his eyes from Bauman and watched the
young rebel climb slowly to his feet, bruises discol-
oring his face, chest, and shoulders. He moved to the
center of the ring and began instructing the class on a
series of karate punches, parries, and kicks. Jihar
then looked back at the woman as she wandered
away from the karate class.

She walked slowly through the walled mountain
village. The buildings were created from dung-
colored stone and seemed to have no glass in any
of the windows. Some of structures were whole with
armed guards standing near the doors. Others of them
lacked roofs or walls, having been hit by bombs.
Others had black streaks near the windows or the
door where fire had touched them. A shattered palm

tree, its broad leaves browned, stood near the ruin of one large building. A massive hole in the side revealed the interior, the two upper-level floors sloping toward the hole. Broken bits of wood, blocks of cement, and stones were scattered on the sand under the hole. A blackened crater marred the surface near the building.

She turned and headed toward the demolitions class. She recognized the instructor as Zabib. He was a short and slender young man with a bony face and broken, yellowed teeth. As she approached, he put his finger through the ring on an igniter and yanked it.

"That is all," he told the class. "You pull the ring." He threw up his hands and grinned at them. "And wait, of course. You must wait."

Bauman glanced at the fuse as it burned with a bright, popping flame and a small cloud of dense, blue smoke. A couple of the young men of the class glanced at one another, almost as if afraid. One of them wiped sweat from his forehead as if he had suddenly realized that he was sweating. His eyes were on the slow-burning fuse. A young woman slid backward on the ground, her eyes locked on the plastic explosive. Bauman turned her attention back to the fuse that was stretched out on the crude table of dirty, stained wood, and wondered how far Zabib would let it go—how far he could *let* it go.

A young man jumped to his feet, his eyes fixed on the burning fuse. One of his friends grabbed his arm and another stood, a hand on his shoulder, trying to force him to sit down, whispering to him. The terrified man jerked his arm away from his friend, turned savagely on the other, and then bolted away, running headlong into Jihar, a scream bubbling in his throat.

He fell to the burning sand, his eyes wide in terror as he stared up at the mountain of a man.

As Jihar lifted the young man to his feet, glaring at him, Zabib snipped the fuse with wire cutters. He tossed the burning fuse to the ground where it sputtered and then died in a puff of blue smoke.

Jihar looked at Bauman and said, "You are surprised, Miss Bauman, that some of our young people have yet to master their fear of death?"

"Why should it surprise me?" she asked, a hint of a German accent in her voice. She began to smile and added, "Not a thing one inherits, is it?"

As she stopped speaking a single rifle shot echoed. She glanced at Jihar, who was looking up at a sentry posted on an overhanging ledge of rock high above the camp. He was waving his rifle and shouting, but his words were lost in the distance, blown away on a hot, desert breeze. He pointed at the sky behind them.

They turned and saw a helicopter approaching. At first just a noiseless speck in the distance, it grew slowly until it was easily identifiable, the sound rippling and building as the aircraft approached. It hovered briefly, kicking up a cloud of sand in its rotor wash. Jihar turned his face away and Bauman turned completely, bending at the waist and wrapping her hands around her cameras to protect them from the stinging sand and whirling dirt.

Two people, Karl Gavril and Maude Wynter, each dressed in khaki, got out and ducked as they ran a few feet until they were clear of the rotor blades. A second later, as the noise increased, the helicopter lifted, swinging in the air only a couple of feet above the sand, spun and climbed with a roar of its engine and a blast of wind and sand.

As soon as the helicopter was gone, the engine noise and the beat of the rotors fading in the distance, Jihar rushed forward, wrapping his arms around Gavril, slapping him on the back.

"Welcome, Gavril. Your presence alone is an inspiration to our movement."

An hour later a half dozen rebels stood under the hot sun, firing at the rusting hulks of tractors, wagons, and a burned-out Ford that stood on the flapping remains of its rubber tires. Around the Ford the ground sparkled as the sunlight was caught and reflected by the shattered glass from the windshield. The bullets from the AK-47s slammed into the vehicles, rocking them with the impact, dust and dirt flying from them, or ricocheting off.

Jihar, Gavril, and Wynter stood to the side, watching the weapons practice. The tall man in a khaki uniform and carrying a long, thin stick wrapped in rawhide ordered a cease-fire, and a second group moved to the firing line, taking the weapons that had been used by the first.

"So tell us, Jihar," said Gavril, grinning broadly, "how may we help you?"

Jihar looked at him probingly, glanced at the AK-47s on the firing line, and then said, "Weapons. Ammunition. Money to finance large-scale assaults."

"You ask a lot, but all this is possible—providing, of course, you and your men are worthy of such a commitment and willing to pay the price for it." He kept his eyes on the men and women on the firing line.

"We are dedicated to that end," replied Jihar quickly and coolly.

"That is what we are here to find out," Gavril shot back.

As Gavril stood silently, Wynter leaned close to him and whispered something in his ear. She pointed toward Bauman, who was photographing the rebels as they practiced with their automatic weapons.

"The woman with the camera." Gavril began gesturing at the photographer.

"Elli Bauman," said Jihar, shrugging. "The massacre of the refugee camps—her photographs of the victims brought us much public support."

"Hans Kroger," Wynter said quietly, watching Bauman. "The magazine article."

"Yes." Gavril nodded as he stroked his chin with his left hand, thinking. "And she covered the trial of the Libyan freedom fighters in Hebron. I remember now."

Much later there was a loud whistle and the demolition class emptied the bleachers, jogging across the baked sand of the compound to the karate class. Jihar and Gavril watched as the classes changed places, the students ignoring everything around them, including the visitors and photographer.

Jihar and Gavril were alone, near a granary that had been converted to a mess hall. They had been inside, further discussing the need for weapons while they had been eating a cold lunch—all kinds of weapons to be used against the government, or against *any*one who opposed them. Neither paid attenton to the flock of pigeons that pranced near the door, pecking at spilled grain. Several of them strayed under the building.

"Then you prove the enemy vulnerable," said Gavril, responding to Jihar's question.

Jihar stopped walking and glared at Gavril. "We are not sufficiently armed for direct confrontation. I have told you this."

Gavril looked up and saw Wynter leave the mess hall, a cat cradled in her arms. Pausing at the door as she gently stroked the animal, she turned and said something to someone behind her. Gavril turned his attention back to Jihar and put a reassuring hand on his arm.

"I do not question your courage, Jihar, but you need weapons." He grinned broadly at some private joke. He nodded and added quickly, "Perhaps America would supply your organization as well."

To one side they heard the pigeons scattering, their wings beating the air. There was a squawking from one of the birds. Gavril turned and saw the cat bounding for the birds trapped under the building.

"Under the right circumstances, perhaps," Jihar agreed reluctantly.

Gavril grinned. He then saw Bauman approaching the demolitions class. He studied her closely for a moment and smiled to himself. "This Elli Bauman. I should meet her."

Wynter ran up to them then, as they walked toward the demolitions class. She slipped her arm around Gavril's waist, clinging to him, pressing a breast against his arm. None of them noticed the cat as it emerged from under the building, a struggling pigeon with a bloodstained wing clamped firmly in its jaws.

CHAPTER TWO

Colonel Charles Halloran sat behind his Marine-issue, battleship gray, metal desk in the Quonset hut that was his headquarters and the headquarters of the First Reconnaissance Battalion. Halloran was a big, burly man with thick hair that was turning gray. He had a thick neck, a square jaw, a long, thin nose and wide-set blue eyes. He had a gravelly voice and rarely had to speak much above a whisper to get his point made. On the wall behind him were recruiting posters showing the Recon Marines in action, storming a beach, parachuting, infiltrating enemy lines, attacking across open ground with bayonets fixed, and rappeling from hovering Huey helicopters. Surrounding the poster were citations and decorations that Halloran had received during his career. On the front of his desk, where his visitors could see it, would have to look at it, was a skull and crossbones centered in a black diamond. The words *Swift. Deadly. Silent. First Reconnaissance Marines* encircled the emblem.

There was a tap at the door and a young Marine clerk centered himself there. He was wearing starched fatigues that showed sweatstains under the arms and down the back. "Sir, Gunnery Sergeant Burns is here to see you."

Halloran kept his eyes on his papers, scribbled his name on the top one, and as he set it aside said, "Send him in, Corporal."

Outside the headquarters hut, Sergeant Manuel Ramirez approached James and Ruggieri, who were also wearing sweatstained fatigues, both newly promoted to corporal. Each was holding a large paintbrush. There were buckets of whitewash near them as they painted the stones lining the base of the hut.

Ramirez bent down, picked up one of the rocks, and checked the bottom. "Corporal Ruggieri."

Ruggieri looked up eagerly. "Yes, Sergeant."

"You see these rocks here? They are the colonel's own rocks. He brought them here himself, from that creekbed over there. I saw him do it." Ramirez dropped the rock and dusted the palms of his hands together.

Ruggieri stared up at him blankly, blinking in the bright sunlight. He glanced at the rock he had been painting, looked at James, who wore a skeptical expression, and then looked back at Sergeant Ramirez.

Ramirez pried another rock loose, exposing its unpainted bottom. He leaned close to Ruggieri, as if to speak to him confidentially. "The colonel likes his rocks painted top, sides, and bottom, Marine."

Ramirez winked at James as Ruggieri turned to look at the long line of rocks that they had painted on the top and sides, but not the bottom.

"You mean we gotta—" started Ruggieri.

James interrupted and said, "Sergeant Ramirez, how come you always messin' with my man here?"

For a moment Ramirez stared down at him, and then burst out laughing. He started on his way, shaking his head, chuckling to himself.

"Shine him on, Ruge," said James. "Ain't nothing but—" He stopped talking and looked up at the window of the Quonset hut, where Halloran stood watching them. He held the colonel's eyes for an instant and then turned his attention back to white-washing the rocks.

Halloran was behind his desk, standing in the window so that he could watch the men outside for a moment. Burns was sitting across from him, in one of the two old leather chairs reserved for visitors. There was a worn carpet on the floor that had faded to gray. A bookcase crammed with Marine Corps manuals stood to one side. A picture of Halloran's family sat on top of the bookcase. Behind him, shoved into a corner, was a round, knee-high table that contained mint copies of various military publications.

"Those two boots finally earned their wings, huh?" said Halloran. He turned to face Burns.

"Yes sir," said Burns, grinning, remembering the recent ceremony. "They finally did."

Halloran moved the chair and sat down behind his desk. He smiled and then said, "I can remember when I earned mine. A boot lieutenant I was. What's it been now? Thirty-four years ago? Goddamn platoon sergeant, big Polack son of a bitch, nearly caved in my chest."

"My father had some stories to tell about that, sir," offered Burns.

Halloran looked at Burns. "Master Sergeant Joseph Burns," he said. He shook his head and added, "He ever tell you the time he and I were on leave in the Philippines?"

"You mean the time he kept you out of the brig, sir?" answered Burns, still grinning.

"He told you that?" asked Halloran, surprised. Then he added sharply, "Horseshit! It was the other way around." Halloran began to chuckle, but it changed to a coughing spasm. When he finally caught his breath, he sighed heavily and looked away momentarily.

"That's not why I called you in here, goddammit," said Halloran, his eyes boring into Burns. He snatched a handful of papers from his desk, and waved them like a banner. "I just received orders. Assigned to Jemal as the Assistant Defense Attaché."

"Sorry to see you go, Colonel," said Burns.

"Yeah, CMC must've figured I was enjoying myself a little too friggin' much here in Recon."

"Where else they gonna pay you for jumpin' outta airplanes, sir?" said Burns.

Halloran ignored the remark and asked, "Did you see today's paper?" He slid it across the desk so that Burns could read the headline: U.S. AGREES TO SELL ARMS TO JEMAL.

"How are the Israelis going to take that?" asked Burns.

"It's a sensitive subject," said Halloran. "Some people think Jemali President Nahir could be on shaky ground. If that happens, who knows where those arms will end up."

"Why send them?"

Halloran leaned back in his chair. It squeaked

loudly. "Their Minister of Finance Amin controls the purse strings in Jemal. You know that game."

"Sounds like a lot of wheeling and dealing to me, sir."

"Nothing new about that. Right, Gunny?"

"Sounds like you'll have your work cut out for you, sir," Burns said.

"Damn right I will," answered Halloran. He hesitated and then grinned. "That's why I'm taking you with me."

"Sir?"

"You heard it right. They got a rebel over there named Abu-Jihar. Big sucker. Trying to stir the people up against the government. Could be a lot of problems. I want you there in charge of Marine security. If the shit hits the fan, you can cover my ass. You don't have a problem with that, do you, Gunny?"

"No sir, Colonel sir."

"It didn't have to be this way," Halloran said quietly.

"You mean I still have a choice, Colonel?"

"You made it when you turned down OCS."

"With all due respect, sir," said Burns, "you know how us Burnses feel about officers."

Halloran glared at Burns.

"Will that be all, sir?" Burns asked stiffly.

"That will be all."

As Burns got to his feet, Halloran reached for a magazine partially obscured by all the papers on his desk. Halloran opened it and said, "Have a nice fucking day, Jack."

Burns stopped at the door, turned to face Halloran. Finally he grinned lopsidedly. "Thank you sir," he said.

Halloran watched him leave, staring at the empty space for just a moment. He then turned his attention to the magazine. On the cover was a picture of Karl Gavril and Maude Wynter dressed in old fatigues, bandoliers across their chests, AK-47s in their hands, and kaffiyeh wrapped around their heads. The caption said, "Ambassadors of Terror Strike in Cyprus."

Burns pulled his white T-Bird convertible across the freeway toward one of the exit ramps for Santa Barbara. He worked his way through the streets until the area changed from commercial buildings to houses. He turned a corner onto a street lined with large houses that were surrounded by tall trees, bushes, and flower gardens. There were well-manicured lawns reaching to the street. Burns pulled into the driveway of a Spanish-style house, a single-story dwelling of imitation adobe with a red tile roof. There were black wrought-iron bars over the windows that were topped with points. He noticed a Mercedes 500 SEC parked on the street in front of the house, the trunk open and a man leaning into it. The man straightened and turned, setting a small duffel bag on the ground beside the rear tire, out of the way.

The man, Rod Drummond, saw Burns and then called, "Jack! How the hell are you?" Drummond was medium height, tan and fit, and although in his early forties, he looked younger. He was wearing polo gear that wasn't fresh, and there were beads of sweat on his forehead.

Burns nodded and said, "Great, Rod."

"Good, good. Dana's drying to see you. Just got back from the polo field. Dana loves the horses."

Drummond laughed self-consciously. "You know how little girls are about horses."

"No, Rod, how are they?" Burns asked sarcastically.

Drummond ignored both the question and the attitude behind it. "Well, come in the house, boy. Helen's bought all kinds of new shit since you were here last."

Drummond picked up his equipment, handed a bundle to Burns, and then headed across the lawn to the massive front door made of dark wood and covered with ornate carvings. He unlocked the door, pushed it open, and then stepped back so that Burns could enter first.

As he stepped in, Drummond yelled, "Helen! Where the hell are you? Jack's here."

From the back of the house they heard a female voice reply, "Coming."

Drummond dropped the gear to the ceramic tile floor, turned, and said, "I'd offer you a beer, Jack, but the taps full out. All you Marines drink is beer, isn't it?"

"Apple juice," said Burns.

"Apple juice?"

"Yeah," Burns said seriously. "You got any apple juice?"

"I don't know," Drummond said. He saw Burns staring at him, but wasn't sure what he could see in the eyes. He couldn't tell if the big Marine was putting him on or if he was serious. He shrugged and said, "I'll go and see."

As Drummond disappeared through one door, Helen entered through another. Thirty years old, tall and slender, she was wearing a light-colored blouse open at the throat and half-unbuttoned, and tight, designer jeans. Her blond hair was swept back and tied behind her head. She stopped in front of Burns, put her hand on his shoulders and kissed him lightly on the cheek, just as a sister might greet a favorite brother.

"Hello, Jack."

"Helen, you're looking good, as always," Burns said, stepping back so that he could see her better.

"You look very fit yourself," she said. She glanced around quickly and asked, "Where's Rod?"

"He went to get me some apple juice."

"Apple juice, huh?" she said, smiling.

"Well, you know we have to stay in shape." He slapped his belly.

"Come on," she said. "We better help him find you your apple juice."

Helen moved down the hall and into the kitchen. Burns followed close behind, watching her back carefully. As they entered the kitchen, they saw Drummond bent over, both doors on the massive refrigerator open. Burns could see the doors lined with eggs, cheese, butter, and nearly every beverage known to the human race. They heard bottles rattling as Drummond pawed through them, searching.

"Can't find a damned thing in here," he said.

"Rod, I'll get it," said Helen, sounding exasperated.

Drummond closed the doors quickly and faced Burns. "Great. I never was comfy in the— What do you guys call it, Jack? The mess?"

"You know how the mess got its name, Rod?" Burns asked.

"No."

"It was way back in 1776, it was. Some asshole

got the Marine cook all pissed off. Seems he was making dumb jokes about the Corps. Well, that cook took out his bayonet," Burns said, picking up a kitchen knife and testing the blade with the edge of his thumb, "and the next thing you know it was *whack, whack, whack.* Blood everywhere. Took 'em days to clean it up. A real mess. They've been calling it the mess ever since."

"I don't know," Rod said quietly, his eyes fixed on the knife. "Hell of a story, though. I'll go see if Dana's ready." He left the kitchen.

"That wasn't very funny," Helen said.

"I guess I'm not very funny anymore."

"You used to be."

Burns stepped close to her and touched her shoulder, staring into her eyes. "Do you think I've changed?"

"No, not you Jack," she said. "That was the trouble, you could never change."

"You once liked it that way, remember?"

Helen hesitated and then changed the subject. "When are you leaving?"

"How did you know I was leaving?"

Helen leaned back against the counter, both hands on the edge. She looked at Burns and said, "I've seen that look too many times before."

"I guess you did."

"Are you going to tell her or—"

Burns cut her off. "I'll tell her," he snapped. "How is she?"

"Misses you. She always misses you."

"Polo," Burns said, shaking his head. "You got her playing polo?"

"Lessons," Helen said quickly, embarrassed. "It's

very big around here with the horsey set. Junior League, Junior Deb, Junior High."

"She's growing up fast."

"Be sure you don't miss it."

Before she could say more, Dana entered. She was twelve years old, a good-looking kid with long hair and long legs. She rushed at Burns, leaping at him. "Daddy! Daddy!"

Burns scooped her up, hugged her, and whirled her around. "Lemme look at my baby. Wow! What a knockout. You ready to do the town with your old man?"

"Ready?" she asked breathlessly. "I've been ready all week."

"All right," said Burns. "You can show me all the local hot spots." He winked at her.

Dana took his arm and almost dragged him from the kitchen, toward the front of the house. Helen followed, opened the front door, and bent so that Dana could kiss her good night. She hugged Dana.

"Bye, you two. Have a good time."

Dana bolted out the door and headed directly for the T-Bird. Burns stepped to the porch and turned to face Helen in the doorway. "I won't get her back too late."

"I know," she said. She hesitated and then added, "Jack, take care of yourself, okay?"

"I will." He looked into her eyes, studying her face for a moment. Then he said, "Well, uh, good-bye, Helen." He turned and started toward the car without waiting for a reply.

For an instant, Helen stood in the door. Before closing it she said, softly, so that he couldn't hear, "Good-bye Jack. You son of a bitch."

* * *

Burns took Dana to the closest McDonald's for their dinner. They carried their McDLTs, french fries, and chocolate shakes outside, and sat under a brightly colored umbrella, the food scattered on the white plastic table. Burns took a huge bite from his sandwich and the sauce dripped down his chin. Dana reached over and wiped it off.

Later they went to a movie—something with a lot of rock music, flashing lights, and little story in it—ate popcorn, and drank Cokes. They left the theater about dusk, their arms around each other, strolling along a pier, listening to the surf lap at the supports. Lights on poles lined the pier, dropping pools of light along it. A tall, slender girl in short white shorts walked by and smiled at Burns. He turned to watch her retreat. Dana elbowed him in the ribs, laughing.

They came to a stairway that led from the pier to the beach below. They walked down and then stopped. Dana sat on the bottom step, took off her shoes, and rolled up her pants. Burns watched and then joined her, taking off his shoes and socks. Together they moved to the tide line, and walked along it, carrying their shoes.

"Oh, Daddy," Dana said. "I had such a good time today. I wish it would never end."

"Me too, baby," he said. "Dana, there's something I want to tell you."

"Don't say it," she commanded, her voice suddenly cold. She refused to look at him as she asked, "You're going away again, aren't you?"

"It's my job."

"Daddy, can I ask you something?" She stopped walking and turned to face him.

"Sure. Anything."

"Is it true you coulda been a general or something?" she asked.

Burns laughed. "Who told you that?"

"I remember hearing Mom say something a long time ago about being an officer and not having to move around so much. That kinda stuff." She spoke quietly, as if sharing a great secret with him.

"Well, let me tell you," said Burns. "When I was a little boy I wanted to be like your grandpa, a Marine sergeant. Your great-grandpa too. So I became a sergeant. I guess there was a time I could have given it up, gone to officers' school, your Mom wanted me to . . . But I couldn't leave my boys, seeing those kids not much older than you, baby face, growing into men," he told her.

"Daddy, I understand."

"You do?"

"Sure," she said. "I wanna be just like my dad, and besides, you'll always be a general to me." She turned and saluted him solemnly. She laughed, spun, and sprinted up the beach. Burns chased her, letting her outrun him for a while. When he caught her, he wished again that it didn't have to end, but knew it did. He had a new assignment that was half a world away.

CHAPTER THREE

Through the tinted glass of the windows of the limousine, Burns could see a crowd of people, young people dressed in a variety of clothes, turbans, sandals, and robes, circling outside the main gate of the American Embassy. A few carried placards, some in English and some in Arabic, and a few in Russian. Beyond the demonstrators was a sandy, three-story building ringed with palms and bright-flowered bushes, protected by a wall topped with barbed wire and shredded glass.

Burns shot a glance at Halloran, but neither man spoke as the limousine slowed to a crawl and inched deeper into the crowd. For a moment, the people moved aside as if to create a path, but then swarmed around the car again, pounding on the trunk and sides, hitting it with cardboard placards that demanded AMERICANS, GO HOME! and spitting on the windshield to show their discontent. They shoved at the sides, rocking the limo on its springs, but none of them stood in front of it, as if afraid they would be run over.

At the gate, the limousine stopped until the Marine guard could swing the wrought-iron out of the way. The car passed through slowly and as the crowd pressed forward, the guard swung the gate shut, stopping the mob from entering the embassy grounds. Several Marines, pistols drawn or carrying riot guns, ran from the main embassy building toward the gate to reinforce the guard there, but the crowd turned and began circling again, renewing their chant.

In the middle of the demonstrators a large man held up an American flag. The people near it reacted with hate, screaming in a variety of languages, shouting obscenities, and picking up the chant of "Americans, go home!" Jihar tried to keep his face a mask of hatred as he set the flag on fire. Around him the demonstrators broke into cheers and chants as the flag burned, held aloft on a metal pole. When the material fell apart and the flag dropped to the ground, the rabble swarmed forward, stomping at it.

Inside the compound, Halloran and then Burns got out of the backseat of the limousine. The driver, a Marine corporal who had opened the door, snapped to attention and saluted Halloran, who refused to look at the crowd as he moved to the door of the embassy. Burns turned long enough to see the flag catch fire. He wanted to order the guards to wade into the sea of demonstrators to rescue the colors, but knew that he could not interfere with the natives outside the grounds of the embassy, no matter what the reason. He clamped his teeth together, the muscles at his jaw knotted. Finally, he jerked his eyes away from the scene and followed Halloran into the embassy.

Upstairs, the members of the Marine Security Force met in a small conference room. Sergeant Ramirez, Corporal James, and Corporal Ruggieri sat in the front row. Behind them were three other Marines, men who had been on the Security Force for the last six months. They were all seated in wooden chairs with arms that flared into desklike projections to hold notepads. At the front of the room was a bulletin board containing various announcements, including a demand that they wear their ribbons properly and proudly, and a list of approved off-duty activities. There was a blackboard on the wall that had been erased but not washed. On one wall was a framed print of the Marines storming the beaches on Iwo Jima.

Ramirez looked at his watch, verified the time with the clock over the bulletin board, and then glanced at the men with him. He said, "Hey, James. Did you get lucky yet?"

"I'm not going after any women who have to hide behind veils," James announced. "Who knows *what's* under there?"

"Hey, man," Ruggieri said, "if they knew you was on the loose, they'd make 'em cover their eyes too."

"I can't wait to get me some of those belly-dancing lessons," Ramirez said.

James leaped to his feet, spun around, wiggling his hips and shuffling his feet. "Hey, Sarge. You want to see moves? I got moves."

Several men laughed and Ruggieri clapped his hands in time to the unheard music. At that moment, the door opened and Burns entered.

James turned, saw Burns, and collapsed back into his chair. He wiped a hand across his forehead as if the exertion had made him sweat.

Burns stared at the corporal for a moment and then said, "That's the best I've seen you move, Corporal, since Recon."

"He was showing us the local steps, Sarge," Ramirez said, grinning.

"Right out of *Flashdance*," added Ruggieri.

"Okay," Burns said, holding up a hand to stop the discussion. He flipped a sheet of paper over the top of his clipboard. "Listen up. It's a little tense out there, so there's a couple of points I want to reiterate to you guys. Since we've been asked to maintain a low profile here, there'll be no leaving the embassy for a few beers while in uniform."

"But, Sarge," Ruggieri said, "how am I gonna impress the ladies without my uniform?"

"Use your magnetic personality, Ruggieri," Burns said, glaring at him.

There was a bark of laughter from the other men, who quickly fell silent.

"And," Burns added, "while we're on the subject, stay away from the local women, unless they're in bars. The Jemalis are sensitive about their women."

"Is that why they hide them?" Ramirez asked, surprised.

"No, Sergeant," Burns answered. "They probably hide them to keep them from getting run over by you." He stared at the younger NCO and then asked, "Did you do a lot of drag racing in high school?"

"As a matter of fact, Sarge, me and my older brother raced every weekend back in Bakersfield," Ramirez said proudly. He looked at the other men as if seeking their approval.

"Well, the colonel doesn't appreciate it much from the backseat of the limo, particularly when he's got Jemalis brass with him."

Ramirez held up a hand and protested, "Honest to God, Gunny, that dude was trying to cut me off."

"I believe you, Leadfoot. Lighten up."

"Ramirez, you're a regular Shirley Muldowney," James said, grinning.

There was another burst of laughter. Ruggieri was nearly doubled over, he was laughing so hard.

"Pay attention," Burns snapped. "There's to be a weapons demonstration for Jemali militia. James, you'll operate the saw automatic; Ruggieri, the M16 and mortar; Roberts, the M203 launcher."

"When's this gonna take place, Gunny?" Ramirez asked, his face burning because of the Shirley Muldowney remark.

"Good question. Soon as the Jemalis move those weapons off the docks. Our people sent them."

"How come we're not in charge?" Ruggieri wanted to know.

"It's their country," Burns said. "We're just observers here. And don't any of you guys forget it."

The cargo boat at the end of the dock rocked gently in the slight swell from the ocean. There were several Jemali militiamen, dressed in heavy khaki uniforms despite the heat of the day, moving large cases from the deck of the ship to a two-and-a-half-ton truck. A young Jemali lieutenant, just out of his teens, watched the men work, shouting an occasional order to them that they seemed to ignore. Gunnery Sergeant Burns stood next to him.

"I hope your government knows how much we appreciate these weapons, Sergeant," the lieutenant said, picking up a grenade launcher from one of the crates near them. He sighted along the barrel and then lowered the weapon. He didn't put it back in the crate.

"As long as you operate and maintain them with loving care, they'll do real well for you, Lieutenant," Burns said.

"We look forward to your demonstrating their full firepower."

The Jemali guards shoved the last crate into the truck, followed it in, and the driver stepped up to slam the tailgate home, locking it. He walked to the front of the truck and climbed up into the cab. Before starting the engine, he leaned out the window and waved at the lieutenant to tell him that everything was ready.

Burns, holding a requisition form, tried to hand it to the Jemali officer, who pretended not to see it.

"Do you mind if I don't sign this until we get to the armory?"

Burns smiled. "Not at all. Would you like to ride up with me?"

"That would be very nice. Thank you."

Burns and the lieutenant got into the jeep. The lieutenant turned and dropped the grenade launcher into the backseat. As the truck started and then moved out from the pier, Burns reached down for the ignition switch of his jeep, cranking its engine. He slammed the jeep into gear, spun the wheel, and took off in the lead with a roar.

They turned away from the sea, along a highway that took them along open desert, an occasional palm or date tree growing near the roadway. As they approached the city, workmen had put up barricades with detour signs pointing into an older section of the city, where the streets were narrow and twisted back on themselves. Burns slowed, turned to follow the sign, and studied the road crew, but saw nothing un-

usual about them. Over his shoulder, he could see
the truck right behind him.

As they drove through the city, the Jemali lieutenant yelled over the roar of the wind caused by the
motion of the jeep, "Tell me, Sergeant. You like rock
'n roll?"

"I'm more into country," Burns said.

"I like rock 'n roll very much," said the lieutenant. "When I went to school in America, I got into
—how do you say? boogeying?"

Burns glanced at him and smiled.

"You think you could get me some cassettes from
the U.S.?" asked the lieutenant. "Like Dire Straits
and Tears for Fears?"

"I'll see what I can do."

As they continued, the streets narrowed and filled
with people. There were street merchants, their
tables erected near the ancient stone archs. Colored
pennants flapped in the breeze and striped awnings
rippled. There were food vendors, some of them
with small carts, yelling. To one side a man had
hung carpets on a wall. Next to him, a man had a
table littered with pots and jars, some made of metal,
some pottery. More than one of the pots was made
from an empty shell casing. People circulated among
the shops and tables, men, women, and children,
each trying to buy or sell something. Dogs ran loose,
barking, and chasing chickens that flapped and
clucked in fear. There was a pole where three goats
were tied, and another where a single cow stood. In
the distance was an outdoor cafe.

Elli Bauman sat in the cafe. There was a cup of
tea in front of her and she lifted it occasionally, but
didn't drink much, nursing it so that she wouldn't
have to buy another cup. On the chair next to her

were her cameras and camera bag. She watched an old fruit peddler as he pushed his overladen cart up the cobblestone street. The old man stopped, slid a wooden wedge under one of the wheels, and then straightened. He plucked an orange from the cart, peeled it, and gave half to a kid who stood near him.

Bauman was still watching when she heard the noise of the jeep turning onto the street. She looked at the American Marine who was driving, and then at the weapons truck behind him. Getting to her feet, she grabbed her camera, moved away from a busboy blocking her, and waited.

Burns slowed and looked back. The truck had managed to make the sharp turn, but had nearly stopped. The people swarmed around it, some holding out hands demanding money, others displaying wares for sale. One man leaped onto the running board and shoved a hand in the window of the cab. A group of young men spilled from a side street, and Zabib, the terrorist who taught demolitions to the rebels, rushed to the truck, slammed into it, and screamed as if in great pain.

The driver jammed on the brakes and the guard in the passenger seat got out to investigate. Burns stepped on his brakes as the crowd surged around the truck and the guard was swept away. Burns passed an alley and stopped, but before he could put the jeep into reverse, a car shot out from the alley and crashed into the stone wall on the other side of the narrow street. There was an explosion of steam as the radiator collapsed.

Burns jumped from the jeep and ran to the door of the car. "You tryin' to kill somebody?" he demanded.

The driver looked as if he didn't understand. He

reached down to open the door, shoving it out of his way, then turned in the seat and pushed a pistol at Burns's stomach. Burns kicked the door shut, catching the man's hand between the frame and the post. He roared in pain and dropped his pistol to the ground. Reaching through the window, Burns grabbed the front of the man's shirt and smashed his elbow into his face. Then he ripped open the door and jerked the man from the seat. He threw him to the street, tensed, and waited for the driver to fight back.

At the truck, the Jemali driver was trying to see if he had injured anyone. He leaned out the open window on his side of the vehicle, trying to see what was happening. Two hands shot from the crowd, seizing the man and dragging him through the window.

Elli Bauman pushed her way through the crowd and was taking pictures as fast as the automatic wind on her camera could advance the film. She switched from the truck driver to the crowd and back again.

By now the Jemali guard had reached the man who had been hit. The man didn't look as if he had been badly hurt and the guard reached down to help him to his feet. Zabib, faking his injuries, smiled at the guard and then jammed a pistol into his face. He fired once and the guard flipped back, blood covering his face. He tried to draw his weapon as his sight failed. He died before he figured out what was happening around him.

Another car appeared behind the truck, scattering pedestrians as it squealed to a halt. A man wearing a hood leaped from the back and opened fire on the rear of the weapons truck with an Uzi. The Jemali guards were tossed around, blood spattering the side of the truck, staining their uniforms and the floor of the vehicle as they died. It all happened so fast that they never fired a shot in return.

With the first shots, people started screaming. They scattered, fleeing the scene, ducking for what little protection was available in the street shops. They dived under tables and behind displays, pushed open doors and ducked down alleyways.

Burns spun when the first shots were fired. He clawed at the .45 on his hip as he ran toward the weapons truck. The Jemali lieutenant leaped to the street to follow, a submachine gun in his hand.

Jihar, who had arrived in the car, held the Jemali driver bent over backward. He pressed a thick arm against the driver's throat, and suddenly snapped the man's head forward. There was a pop of bone and the driver went limp, dying. Jihar let him fall to the ground, stepped over the body, and climbed into the cab of the deuce and a half. He tossed the Uzi he carried into the seat beside him.

The door on the other side opened, and Zabib leaped in. He glanced over at Jihar, who wheeled the truck around, scattering the remaining crowd. Zabib grabbed the Uzi from the seat beside Jihar and pointed it out the window, firing a long burst, smashing pots and shattering a couple of wooden tables.

The Jemali lieutenant had drawn his own weapon and was racing down the street toward the truck as it started to move. He saw the barrel of the Uzi pointed at him. He tried to raise his own weapon, but the burst of fire stitched him across his chest and he tumbled to the ground, his blood pooling under him, staining the cobblestones of the street. He tried to sit up once, saw the blood on the front of his uniform and collapsed, dying as his head hit the ground.

Burns aimed his .45, squeezing the trigger. Around him, the pottery exploded as the slugs from the rebels' weapons ricocheted. Burns rolled to the right and came up firing again. The truck rocked and then lurched around a corner, out of range. Right behind it was the car carrying the rest of the ambushers. One of them leaned out the window to fire at Burns, who aimed his own weapon carefully and shot back. The rounds struck the man in the face and chest. He dropped his Uzi and pitched out the window, rolling over in a cloud of dust.

There was a sound behind him and Burns spun, saw the rebel who had crashed the car running toward him. The man fired a quick shot that was wide. Then, suddenly, he whirled and ran down the alley, away from Burns.

Burns raced for his jeep, saw the body of the Jemali lieutenant lying in the street, obviously dead. There was too much blood, too many bullet holes. Burns leaped into his jeep and started the engine. He jammed it into gear, spun the wheel, and then slammed on the brakes, his path blocked by a pushcart loaded with fruit. The vendor was trying desperately to move it, pushing against the handles. Finally he gave it a mighty shove, grunting with the effort, and thrust it out of the way. Burns roared by as the fruit tumbled to the street.

Bauman, who had been photographing the whole incident, raised her camera to shoot again, but didn't. She lowered the camera slowly, a look of horror spreading across her face. She dropped the camera and broke into a run. She knelt beside the fruit vendor, who was bent over the kid he had given the orange to. He glanced at her in anger as he held the boy who had been hit by a stray bullet.

Bauman tore a strip of cloth from her dress. "Get a doctor, someone!" she demanded as she tried unsuccessfully to bandage the wound.

In the narrow alley, Burns was chasing the rebel from the crashed car. The man was running, glancing over his shoulder and firing wildly behind him without looking. Burns's eyes were on the back of the man. He was swerving the jeep to miss the obstacles in the alley, gaining on him.

In front of running man was a gap in the solid wall of buildings, a narrow place where he could escape from the madman in the jeep, a haven marked by a patch of sunlight. He turned slightly and fired a last shot at Burns.

Just as the man was about to leap clear, into the narrow passage, Burns swerved and clipped him with the bumper of the jeep. The man was lifted by the force of the impact, cartwheeled in the air, and slammed into the side of a stone building. He slid down it until he was lying prone in the alley. As Burns backed up, the man didn't move.

Burns swerved back into the alley, dropped the jeep into a lower gear, and pushed the accelerator to the floor. The engine roared with power. He shot down the alley, slowing for a corner. As he turned it, the jeep rocked up onto the left-side wheels, but then crashed back to the road, bouncing wildly as Burns shifted again. Far in front of him he could see the weapons truck.

In the truck, Zabib was bouncing high. He slapped a hand to the dashboard and screamed his enthusiasm. He looked at Jihar and then shouted again.

Jihar glanced at him out of the corner of his eyes, downshifted, and hit the accelerator. The truck leaped forward, just making the gap between a bus and a taxi. The drivers of both those vehicles tried to miss the truck and hit each other in an explosion of metal and steam.

Behind them, the car was forced wide, trying to avoid the steaming wrecks of the bus and taxi, whose drivers were now on the street shouting angrily at each other. The rebel car driver yanked the wheel, leaped the curb and plowed into a cafe. The diners and the waiters dived for cover as the car smashed into tables and chairs, bouncing wildly. It crashed through a vine-covered lattice at the end of the cafe, rocked onto two wheels, bounced, and hit the road, the tires screaming in protest. It shot forward as the driver jerked the wheel to the right, trying to steady the car.

The car caught up to the truck, falling in line behind it. The two vehicles roared down the road, the sounds of their engines echoing in the narrow streets, turned, doubled back, and turned again until they were on a tiny road that led out into the desert. They passed a large sand dune that had a single camel with a rider. Behind him a plume of dust was visible— first, just a hint of dust swirling in the bright blue of the afternoon sun, but it became thicker, easier to see. The single rider was joined by another and another, all of them galloping along the edge of the dune, then joined by women on foot, by pack animals and goats, all of them running as if fleeing a monster that was chasing them.

Jihar glanced at the dune, the people on it, and the dust cloud behind it. Suddenly, over the top of it, he saw a jeep, a lone man driving. The jeep hit the sand, the wheels digging in, throwing sand out behind. The driver spun the wheel, angling at the road.

Jihar jammed his foot down against the metal of the floorboard, urging the truck forward. He leaned against the steering wheel and then looked to the side, wondering if the madman in the jeep was going to ram him. He looked to the road and back at the jeep, almost able to see the eyes of the lunatic driving it.

Burns, one hand on the wheel and the other on the gearshift, plowed through the sand toward the road. He watched the truck and the trailing car intently. The gap between them was closing, the racing jeep beginning to catch the heavier and slower weapons truck.

Zabib saw the jeep close, picked up the Uzi, and leaned out the window, trying to sight on the jeep and driver. He braced himself against the side of the truck's window and fired a short burst, but had no idea where the rounds went. There was no effect on the jeep and he fired again, but the truck was swaying and bouncing too much and Zabib couldn't steady his aim. He leaned back inside to switch magazines.

Beside him, Jihar tried to push the accelerator through the floor. He shot a glance out the window, saw the jeep almost on top of him, but didn't waver. He kept his foot pressed hard on the accelerator.

Burns saw that it wouldn't be easy to catch the truck. It was too far ahead of him. He jerked the wheel to the right, hit the hard surface of the road, and slammed into the car of rebels. The car veered sharply from the road, into the sand, setting up a cloud of dust as it spun around and momentarily disappeared from sight.

Burns fought the wheel, got control of his jeep, and fell in line behind the truck. He shifted quickly, floored the gas pedal, and raced forward, gaining on the rebels in the truck. He kept his eyes locked on it, only occasionally glancing at the rearview mirror. In the mirror, he saw the snout of the car emerge from a cloud of dust. It rocketed forward, out of the sand and onto the pavement.

Again Burns was gaining on the truck. He saw a man lean out of the passenger's side and aim a short-barreled weapon at him. Burns slowed slightly and swerved back to use the truck as cover. He heard the hammering of a submachine gun and saw a couple of rounds strike the pavement, whining away. In the rear, the car was gaining on him and a rebel leaned out the window, firing his pistol forward. The windshield of the jeep snapped and a network of lines snaked out from the bullet hole there. Burns whipped the wheel to the left and flew down a side road as the rebel car passed him.

Whipping the steering wheel back to the left, he climbed the bank of sand that led up to the road and flew over the shoulder. The jeep left its wheels momentarily, crashed back to the hard surface, and bounced. Burns fought the wheel, twisted, and the jeep straightened, its tires smoking as they bit the pavement. He downshifted, hit the accelerator, and began to gain on the car and truck.

The rebel in the passenger's seat of the car leaned out to fire at Burns with his pistol. He steadied himself, his arm braced against the side of the car. He fired once, but Burns ducked and veered to the side of the road, out of range of the rebel.

Ahead of them the road curved onto a high bridge. Burns kept the pressure up, gaining on the rear of the car, forcing it to speed up. The driver tried to stay ahead of him, but the truck was slowing to take the curve. It rolled out onto the bridge.

The car's driver didn't slow at first, and then was too close to the truck, forced to slow. Burns kept his foot pressed to the floor, gaining on the car. Without taking his eyes from the road, he reached into the back of the jeep where the Jemali lieutenant had thrown the grenade launcher. One-handed, he aimed it over the top of the windshield. The jeep lurched once and the barrel of the weapon slid to the right, but Burns eased it back until it was pointed at the car again. He hesitated, then pulled the trigger. He felt the weapon recoil as it fired the 40mm grenade. He dropped the empty grenade launcher to the floor of the jeep, his eyes on the fleeing terrorist car.

A moment later there was an explosion of white phosphorus that lifted the rear of the car, flipping it end over end. The trunk popped up and a door flew open as the car crashed back to the bridge, wedging itself against the metal supports, blocking the roadway. One of the rebels danced from the wreckage, staggered away from the car, and then collapsed. Another of them escaped the wreckage, his clothes on fire. He tried to leap the railing, failed and collapsed onto the roadway, the flames covering him from head to foot.

Burns jammed on his brakes, downshifted, and skidded, his jeep slipping sideways toward the burning car. He tried to spin the steering wheel but the tires refused to grip the road and he couldn't control the skid. The jeep slid to a halt touching the rear of the flaming car. Burns threw up an arm to protect himself from the heat, leaped from the driver's seat, ran across the bridge, and dived into the river below.

As he jumped, the gas tank of the car exploded, engulfing it and the jeep in flames that brushed Burns.

Burns surfaced a moment later. He was covered with mud, his hair hanging in his face. He glanced to the burning vehicles on the bridge and then looked at the truck. It was disappearing down the desert road, a plume of dust behind it.

CHAPTER FOUR

Corporal Ruggieri was the Marine on duty. He sat in a small room with a bank of TV monitors in front of him. He let his eyes roam from one to the next. They showed him the area just outside the embassy, the approaches to the front doors, and a couple of the ground-floor hallways. He turned when the door behind him opened.

Ramirez entered carrying a newspaper. Silently, he unfolded it and handed it Ruggieri. "Have you seen this, Ruge? Gunny made the papers *big!*"

Ruggieri looked at the front page. There was a photograph of Burns battering the rebel who had crashed his car, another of him firing his pistol at the truck, a third of Burns smashing his jeep into the car that blocked him, trying to get around it, and a final one of Burns rounding the corner as the fruit cart spilled. Below the pictures, in bold print, was the name of the photographer: Elli Bauman.

"All right!" Ruggieri said, nearly shouting. "Gunny don't take no shit." He pointed to the top photo, the one where Burns was hammering on the rebel. "Look at him wastin' this dude."

"I wish I was there," said Ramirez. "Boy, would I love to see some action, kick some ass."

"Shit, Sarge, I bet you haven't seen no action since you was in East L.A. last."

"Hey, them home boys don't mess with this gyrene," said Ramirez, tapping himself on the chest. "I'm bad, bad."

"You as bad as Gunny?" asked Ruggieri.

"Shit!" Ramirez said, shaking his head. He glanced at the series of photographs on the front page of the paper. "Ain't nobody that bad."

Another copy of the paper lay on a huge, mahogany desk. It was centered on a green felt blotter, where a small lamp with a bright green shade was throwing a pool of light on it. There was a pen and pencil holder near it, a wooden out box, a small glass-enclosed clock, and a color photo of a woman, a boy, and a girl in a leather frame.

The ambassador, Virgil Morgan, sat in his black leather judge's chair, staring at the newspaper. Morgan was a career diplomat, about fifty, who was waiting for a better posting. He had gray hair and bushy, gray eyebrows. He had a thick face and a large nose, cold, steely eyes, and a pointed chin. He had a slender frame, wide shoulders, and the beginnings of a potbelly. He was dressed in a dark blue, three-piece suit, white shirt, and red tie.

Burns was sitting in one wingback chair, his eyes on the ambassador. Halloran was in the other, trying to read the newspaper on the desk. Burns took a deep breath and said, "What the hell did you expect me to do? I wasn't there to direct traffic."

The ambassador looked up from his paper. He studied the Marine for a moment and then glanced to his right at the bookcases that lined one wall from floor to ceiling, containing thousands of brightly colored books that no one ever read. Behind the Marine was a large window that showed the tops of the sand-colored buildings across the street from the embassy, a view that looked more like a picture painted on the wall. Thick drapes lined the windows and would be drawn to keep the late afternoon sun out of the office.

"You were there as an observer," said the ambassador. "Not to engage in any action."

"Those assholes murdered three people, including that kid lieutenant," Burns said, his voice rising and the anger blazing in his eyes. "And ripped off all those weapons. Was I just supposed to observe that?"

"Exactly," said the ambassador. "At no time were you ever given orders to pursue hijackers through the streets and countryside of Jemal, endangering its citizens." He grabbed the newspaper and smacked it back to the desk top. "Just look at this!"

Burns put his hands on the arms of the chair and leaned forward. He started to say something, but then caught sight of Halloran out of the corner of his eye and sat back. He turned his attention to the bookcases.

"Virgil," Halloran said reasonably, his voice quiet, "in all fairness, he was never given orders *not* to pursue, either."

The ambassador stood, the newspaper still in his hand. "Then I'm giving them now," he snapped. He stopped moving, looked at Burns, sighed, and said, "Sergeant Burns, have I made myself clear?"

Burns hesitated, glowered at the ambassador, and then shot a glance at Halloran.

"Burns is a combat-trained war vet, Virgil," said Halloran. "He was in Vietnam when it started. Still there when we pulled out. You develop certain, ah, instincts in combat."

"Then he'll just have to curb those instincts." He faced Burns for a moment and then returned his attention to Halloran. "Something like this could lead to an international incident. Then it's my ass on the line." He came around to the front of his desk, and waited until Burns and Halloran stood. "I think that will be all, gentlemen."

Halloran and Burns moved toward the door. Burns leaned forward to open it for the colonel.

"Unless Sergeant Burns has any further questions," added the ambassador.

"You've made your position clear, Virgil," Halloran said. "Very clear." He exited.

Burns, however, stopped in the doorway and turned back to face the ambassador. "One question, Mr. Morgan," he said, his voice flat, unemotional. "Should I bother to get their license number next time?"

The ambassador returned the stare, but didn't say anything in response.

Burns didn't wait long for a reply. He turned and stepped into the outer office. The dark-haired secretary was at her desk. She was friendly with all the embassy staff, but would let no one crash the ambassador's office without an appointment. She was in her mid-thirties. Burns knew her age because she had told him. He had been surprised, thinking that she was ten years younger. He had also learned that she was not one to be bluffed.

Neither Burns nor Halloran said anything to her. They just walked by, opened the door that led to the corridor, and stepped out. Halloran didn't speak as Burns joined him. Together, they walked down the hall toward the elevator. Burns leaned forward and pressed the down button. A moment later the doors opened and a man and woman, the man in an Air Force uniform and the woman in a light green dress, got off and passed the two Marines without glancing at them.

As they got on the elevator, Halloran said, "You're making it awful tough on yourself, Gunny. And for me too, goddammit!" He pushed the button for the first floor, and glanced at the numbers above the door.

"Colonel," Burns snapped, "what the guy wants is a rent-a-cop. Since when does the Marine Corps—"

"Now look," said Halloran, a hard edge to his voice. "I don't wanna hear that crap either. You know goddamn well how I feel about this turn-the-other-cheek bullshit. But what you don't do is get into a pissing contest with the ambassador."

For a few seconds, neither of them spoke. They stared at one another, waiting. Then, as the elevator slid to a stop, Halloran grinned slightly. "You leave that to me." The doors opened silently and they left the elevator.

"I'll leave that to you, sir," Burns said, a lopsided grin on his face. He hesitated and then added, "Oh, there is just one other thing."

"What's that?"

"I would like to know what that photographer was doing there."

"You're in charge of security around here," Halloran said, clapping Burns on the shoulder. "Find out. Tactfully." He let his hand fall to his side and started toward the electronic door of the embassy foyer, where Sergeant Ramirez waited.

* * *

The jangling of the phone caught her by surprise. Elli Bauman let it ring again, then moved to it and picked it up. "Hello?"

"This is Gunnery Sergeant Jack Burns, Miss Bauman. I'm with the American Embassy here in Jemal."

Bauman picked up the whole phone and carried it toward the balcony where she could hear the Muslim summons to prayer. She set the phone down. "I know who you are, Sergeant," she said. Outside, she could see a bearded muezzin cry out in Arabic, calling to the faithful. He was standing on a tiny balcony on the tower of a nearby mosque. She cradled the receiver between her shoulder and her ear. She turned back to the room and picked up a stack of photos, thumbing through them as they talked. "I'll be more than happy to show you what I have, Sergeant, but I doubt they will be of any—"

She listened to him for a moment, nodding slightly. She wasn't sure exactly what the Marine wanted from her, but was convinced that it had very little to do with the pictures that she held. She heard Burns suggest that they meet at a nearby restaurant and nodded to herself.

As she pulled out the ones that showed the faces of Jihar and Zabib and nodded again unconsciously, she said, "Certainly. I'll meet you there." She cradled the phone and picked up the incriminating photos. She carried them to her bureau drawer, pushed her clothes out of the way, slid her loaded snub-nosed revolver to the side, and hid the pictures there. She closed the drawer.

She moved back to the center of the room, looked out the window again, and then sat down on the edge of the bed. There was a small table and two chairs near the window, a dresser to one side, and a combination desk-and-luggage-rack under a large mirror opposite the bed. For a few minutes, she didn't move. She just listened to the sounds drifting on the desert breeze and watched the ceiling fan rotate slowly. She could feel the perspiration on her forehead, along her upper lip, down her back. Finally she stood, grabbed her purse, and left the hotel room.

She took the elevator to the ground floor and walked through the lobby, ignoring the people at the desk, the pile of luggage near them, and the doorman who stood near the entrance. She walked slowly through the marketplace, taking her time, examining the fruits in one stand, the silks in another, the pottery of a third. She glanced at her watch periodically and then hurried through the market to a cafe nearby.

The inside was dim. There was a small group playing bouzouki music quietly. Potted palms ringed the room and stood near the pointed arcs that separated sections of the room from one another. There was a long bar at one end, and almost opposite was an empty booth. Bauman took that, slipping deeper into the shadows, ordered a drink, and waited. A moment later, the waiter set the glass in front of her and disappeared again.

Bauman sipped her drink, made a face as the alcohol burned her throat, and set it down. As she glanced up, she saw Burns. He turned toward her and slid into the booth with her without speaking.

"Exactly one half hour, Sergeant," she said, checking the tiny watch on her wrist. "You're right on time."

"I've had seventeen years of practice, Miss Bauman."

"Call me Elli, please," she said, smiling slightly. "And, do I call you Sergeant?"

"It's Jack."

"Jack, hum," she said softly. "Jack. A good strong name. Right to the point.'

The waiter reappeared. Burns looked up at him, then to Bauman. He saw that she had a drink. "Would you like a refill?" he asked.

"I'm fine."

Burns turned his attention to the waiter. "Jack Daniel's, on the rocks."

As the waiter left, Bauman took a package of photographs from her purse and slid them across the table to Burns. She held her hand on top of the package for an instant, as if trying to decide whether or not to let Burns to see them. Finally she said, "I expect you wanted to see these?"

Burns picked up the envelope and sorted through the pictures slowly, studying them carefully. He saw that there were shots of him in a number of them, he saw one of the Jemali lieutenant before he was cut down by the rebels, a couple of the truck before it was hijacked, and a number that showed people fleeing the firefight, or trying to hide from it. There was even one of the crashed car, but there were none that showed the terrorists or their getaway vehicle.

When Burns didn't react, Bauman said, "I'm sorry if there's nothing there you can use."

Burns held the pictures in both hands, as he searched through them again. He tapped one stack against the other and asked, "How is it you got such good pictures of me, the Jemalis, and the crowd, and not one clear head shot of any of the hijackers?"

"There was a lot going on," she said, shrugging.

"And how did you happen to be there?"

"I didn't just happen to be there," she said. "I was invited."

"By whom?'

"I can't tell you that."

"People lost their lives."

"People are dying every day in the Middle East," she shot back. "Some from poverty, some from war."

"And you're exploiting it."

"Reporting it," she said. "There's a difference."

Burns dropped the photos to the table and stared into her eyes. "Just whose side are you on?"

"This isn't the Old West, Jack," she responded. "It's not that simple."

"What's simple to me, Miss Bauman, is that these terrorists will use anyone, man, woman, child, to fight their war. And right now they're using you."

"It seems to me that it's your country who fights a war of words," she said accusingly.

"That may be true, Miss Bauman," Burns said. He slid out of the booth and stood up. "Just don't get us mad," he warned her. He stared at her for a moment and then repeated the warning: "Don't get us mad."

He reached into his pocket, pulled out a couple of worn, brightly colored bills, and dropped them on the table to pay for the drinks, hers and the one that he had ordered but never gotten. He left her sitting in the bar, her half-finished drink in front of her.

The black embassy limousine sat at the bottom of the driveway. Sergeant Ramirez was outside of it, tying a small American flag to the radio antenna. He wiped a sweaty hand on the side of the trousers and tried again. He didn't hear Halloran approach.

"Come on, Ramirez," Halloran said, "or we'll be late."

"Yes sir, Colonel." Ramirez looked at the flag and the tiny ties on the end of it. He shrugged, folded it quickly, and jammed it into his pocket. He moved to the rear of the car and opened the door for the colonel.

As Halloran ducked his head to enter, he heard a voice behind him. "Colonel? Colonel?"

Halloran straightened up and turned. He could see the young man who was employed as a cook and houseboy by the embassy. "What is it, Hamed?"

"Will the colonel be home for dinner tonight?" he asked. "Should I prepare anything?"

"No, that won't be necessary. I'll be late tonight."

Hamed ducked his head, almost in a bow. "Just as you say, Colonel." He kept his eyes lowered so that Halloran wouldn't see the hate in them.

Halloran turned and climbed into the car. Ramirez glanced across the roof at the other man, shrugged, and got behind the steering wheel. He started the engine, slipped it into gear, and drove through the gate, waving at the Jemali guard who stood there.

As they turned onto the street in front of the embassy, Ramirez said, "Begging your pardon, sir?"

Halloran had a briefcase open on the seat next to him. He was sorting through the papers. Without looking up, he said, "What is it, Ramirez?"

"Something about that kid I don't like," he said, glancing into the rearview mirror to see if Halloran was paying attention.

"Like what?"

"His eyes."

"What about them?" Halloran shifted the papers to his left hand and looked at the mirror now.

"My grandfather, on my mother's side, back on the reservation . . . he was a shaman."

"A medicine man?"

"That's right, Colonel." He glanced into the mirror again and saw Halloran was smiling. "You can laugh if you want, Colonel, but my grandfather would tell ya that death stalks behind those eyes." Ramirez crossed himself and then concentrated on his driving.

"I didn't know you were so superstitious," said Halloran, still grinning.

"Sure am, Colonel. That's why I keep this little flag my mom made me right here in my pocket."

Halloran laughed and turned back to his papers. They took a corner, the car rocking on its springs and the tires squealing. Halloran didn't even look up from his papers, merely said, "Slow it down, Ramirez."

"Yes sir. Sorry sir. I thought that you were in a hurry."

"I am in a hurry, but not to my own funeral," Halloran said, trying to conceal a grin.

Ramirez shot another glance into the rearview mirror, but Halloran was still working on his papers. He looked back to the street. An Arab woman, a veil hiding her face, appeared in front of the car. She looked neither right nor left, as if oblivious to everything around her. Ramirez hit the brakes: the car fishtailed, the front end dropping, but he couldn't stop it. The woman, frozen in panic, stood rooted to the street, and was struck, the thud of her body against the metal clearly audible.

Halloran dropped his papers, put an arm out to

brace himself against the front seat, and snapped, "Goddammit, Ramirez! I told you to be careful." He jerked on the handle of the car door, threw it open, and leaped out. The woman was lying in the dust, facedown, not moving. Halloran rushed to her as Ramirez opened his door.

From nowhere a small crowd began to gather. Halloran crouched by the woman, looked up at Ramirez, and gently tried to roll her over, being careful not to aggravate her injuries. As he looked into her face, a face that he had seen on the cover of a magazine months earlier, he realized that it was a trap. He let her go, but then saw the pistol in the hand of a grinning Karl Gavril.

Halloran jumped back and kicked out, catching Gavril in the hand. Gavril lost his grip on the weapon and it flew off, landing in the dust. Three men broke from the crowd, blocking Halloran's retreat to the car. Halloran spun so that his side was to them, watching them carefully, waiting for one of them to make a move. His hands were up, protecting his face and neck from the three men.

Ramirez, seeing that, jumped forward, his fists clenched. Up on the balls of his feet, ready to attack, he moved toward the three men in front of Halloran. Suddenly, he was struck on the back of the head, the pain a bright flash of white exploding behind his eyes. He started to put out his hands to break the fall, then collapsed facedown in the dust.

Halloran saw the sergeant hit, but could do nothing about it as Ramirez fell to the ground unconscious. One of the men stepped closer. Halloran feinted with his right hand, and kicked with his foot, clipping the man in the knee. There was a shriek, like tires on dry concrete, and the man fell to his side, his hands around his knee. He rocked from side to side, moaning continually.

The other two men attacked then. Halloran turned to meet them. He kicked once, missed, and stepped forward to regain his balance. He punched, had the blow blocked, punched again, and then kicked, hitting one of the men in the side. The terrorist fell against the car, moaned, and slipped to the ground as Halloran attacked the last of the men, kicking twice and punching, driving him to the rear.

The man danced back, out of the way, drawing Halloran with him. He blocked two punches, came forward, kicking, and then halted as Halloran blocked his blows.

For an instant the two men stood facing one another, Halloran breathing heavily, not used to the heat of the desert. He feinted toward the man and was about to attack again when he was hit from behind. He fell to his knees and two of the men grabbed his arms, preventing him from falling to his face.

They lifted Halloran up, and dragged him to a van standing close by, where they tumbled him into the back. A moment later, Zabib and another of the terrorists carried Ramirez to the van, tossed him in beside Halloran, slammed the doors, and locked them. Two of them climbed into the cab, started the engine, and roared away. The other terrorists, including Gavril, disappeared, rushing back to their cars hidden in the side streets and alleyways. The people who had come from their houses and shops to watch the fight began to drift away, almost as if nothing had happened. In less than a minute after Ramirez had hit the "woman," everyone was gone and only the empty limousine was left behind, its doors open and its motor running.

CHAPTER FIVE

The prison was a huge, walled structure made of ochre stone with dozens of barred windows. At the corners were blockhouses encircled with broken glass, topped by giant spotlights. Armed guards stood on the top of the walls or walked along railings, watching the bare ground below them. Each guard carried either a high-powered rifle or a shotgun. There was a single, wide gate with a bright light above it and thick iron bars across it. There were half a dozen police cars parked outside, along with a single jeep from the American Embassy.

Burns stood in an almost bare room in the prison. Two Jemali soldiers stood by the door, but they were not participating in the questioning. Hamed sat in the only chair, his butt on the front edge, his feet flat on the floor, and his shoulders touching the back. He clasped his hands in his lap and stared at a bright light shining in his eyes. He blinked rapidly, pretending the light didn't bother him. He stared at the floor near his feet and waited.

"Okay, Hamed. Run it by me again," Burns said. He had moved so that he stood over Hamed, looking down at him, but not in the light.

"I've already told you, Sergeant," he said, glancing up at the shadowy shape of Burns. He started to raise his hand to block the light, but thought better of it. He then lowered his eyes again and added, "The colonel said he wouldn't be home for dinner, then they rode off. That's all he said."

"Which direction did he go?"

"The same way they always go." Hamed looked to the two Jemalis, who were barely visible on the outside of the circle of light, as if asking them for help. Neither of them acknowledged him or even moved.

"Did you see anyone follow? Notice any other cars in the street that didn't belong there?"

Hamed turned his head so that he was staring up at the shape of Burns. He wiped a hand across his forehead, looked at the sweat smeared there, and then dried it on his shirt. "I noticed nothing," he said.

Burns stepped in front of Hamed, no longer caring if he was blocking the light, and stared down at him. "Why don't I believe you?"

"I don't know."

"You know Abu-Jihar?"

"I know of him."

"That's all you know? Of him?" Burns asked quickly, giving Hamed no time to think, no time to form a defense. "Nothing else. You just know *of* him?"

"Yes," Hamed said, nodding. "Like everyone else I read about him."

"Didn't you know him at the university?" Burns shot back at him.

"The university?"

"Yeah, the university," Burns said, leaning forward, his hands on the back of the chair, on either side of Hamed's shoulders, his face inches from Hamed's. He was so close that their noses nearly touched, and Burns could smell Hamed's bad breath.

"Well . . ." Hamed said, stalling for time. His head hurt and he needed time to think.

"You were in his classes."

"That was so," Hamed agreed quickly. He raised his hand and rubbed his chin. His eyes held Burns's eyes for a moment and then he looked away.

"Did you ever participate in any of his demonstrations?"

"No, never. I—"

"Bullshit!" snapped Burns. He grabbed Hamed by the front of the shirt and lifted him out of the chair. He shook the smaller man, snapping his head back and forth. "I've got pictures of you parading in the streets with Abu-Jihar. Tell you what, Hamed. We're going to put your ass in a cell for a while for you to think this over. Maybe your memory will get better back there."

"You can't make me say lies," protested Hamed. "I know nothing. But if I did, I wouldn't tell you." He looked at Burns defiantly. He pursed his lips, his eyes blazing in the bright light, and spit directly in Burns's face.

Burns grabbed Hamed by the throat with his massive hands, squeezing, squeezing. He lifted him clear of the chair until his toes just touched the floor. He watched Hamed's eyes grow big and round and white. Hamed gagged, trying to breathe, his fingers clawing at Burns's wrists. He tried to kick, but his feet missed their targets. Burns dropped him back to the chair. He turned away from Hamed and said, "Throw him in a cell."

The van containing Halloran and Ramirez worked its way through a variety of alleyways and back streets, some of them so narrow that the doors of the van were only inches from the walls of buildings, and the pedestrians had to flatten themselves in doorways to let the van pass. The colored awnings on a couple of the shops dragged across the top of the van. They reached the outskirts of the city, passing single-story huts of cinder block with corrugated tin roofs held down by old tires and chunks of stone. There were some trees, mostly palm or rubber, and a few bushes covered with bright blossoms. The ground around the huts was littered with trash, decaying garbage, and broken bits of building materials.

Two women were walking along the edge of the road carrying bundles of food. They glanced at the van as it passed, but quickly shifted their eyes back to the ground, not wanting to see anything or anyone out of the ordinary. They gained an intense interest in the gravel under their feet.

The ground around the road opened up then. Ramshackle huts created out of scrap lumber, broken cinder blocks, and pieces of stone dotted the countryside. Some had pens made of old lumber and palm trunks near them. Others had bright lights from lanterns shining from the doors and windows. There was only a hint of green among all the tans and browns, an occasional vine growing up the side of a hut or on a stone wall, or a date tree standing by itself.

They passed a man at the side of a hut, holding a rope to the head of a camel. He was trying to get the animal to move, but the camel stood as if rooted to the spot. The man beat a long, thin stick against the camel's side, producing no effect whatsoever in the recalcitrant animal.

Not far away, a group of boys kicked a soccerball in the street. One of them booted it into the air, kicked it high with the side of his foot, and then hit it with the top of of his head as if scoring the winning goal. As another of the boys caught the ball, the first stopped moving and watched as the rebel van cruised by.

The road curved and they entered another built-up area. Short buildings of one, two, or three stories lined the street. There were no sidewalks but there were dozens of intersecting alleyways. Some were narrow with a low arch, while others were wide. The van rolled past a number of closed shops, places with faded and torn awnings and windows that were boarded up against vandals and thieves. Signs in Arabic were painted on the front of them. They slowed, took a corner, and pulled to a stop in an alley behind one of the larger buildings.

The engine coughed and died and the driver got out. A moment later the van's rear doors opened. One of the terrorists reached in and grabbed the unconscious Ramirez's feet, dragging him to the edge of the van. Another man reached in, snagged one of Ramirez's arms, and lifted him into a sitting position. The two of them got him out of the van, and then one of them threw him over a shoulder in a fireman's carry and disappeared into the building.

A third man reached in to grab Halloran, who kicked out at him. Another pointed a pistol into the van. When Halloran saw that, he stopped struggling and got out slowly. He was surrounded by terrorists, the man with the gun screened from him. At that moment, Halloran kicked, knocking one of the rebels to the dirt. Another grabbed for him, but his hand slipped and he ripped the gold wings from Halloran's chest.

Halloran was grabbed from behind, a man wrapping his arms around him, holding him. Halloran kicked out again, missed the mark, and tried again. He felt the heel of his boot connect with a shin. There was a grunt of pain. The arms holding him loosened. Halloran grabbed the man's arm, swung his hip into his captor, and flipped him. The man landed on his back. Halloran kicked up, snapping his head back. The man slumped to the ground, unconscious.

Halloran spun to face another terrorist, but found himself looking down the barrel of a pistol. He froze then, his hands out, palms down. He let them subdue him and lead him up a flight of stairs.

Elli Bauman, dressed in her normal uniform of bush jacket and short khaki skirt, descended the stairs to the hotel lobby. She was between two men, both dressed in khaki and wearing kaffiyeh. She had her camera slung over her shoulder and was wearing wide-lens mirrored sunglasses. They crossed the lobby quickly, ignoring all the people there, went through the doors, and stopped at the curb, where a car waited. She halted and waited while one of the men opened the rear door. He got in first and Bauman followed. The other man got in then, sitting beside her, and closed the door. The driver leaned forward, started the engine, and pulled out into the traffic.

As they passed an old fruit peddler who was lean-

ing against the open window of a produce truck talking to the driver, one of the rebels removed Bauman's sunglasses, setting them on his knees. He
reached down for a gauze pad and taped it over Bauman's left eye; the man on her other side did the
same thing. When they had finished, they put her
sunglasses back on so that anyone seeing her from
outside the car wouldn't know that she was blindfolded.

Amin, the Jemali Minister of Finance, was in a
second-floor room in the tenement building. The
room was sparsely furnished. A table with two chairs
stood near the center of it. A pitcher and a glass sat
on the table. The floor was made of bare wood and
covered with a coating of dirt. Bits of paper, tin
cans, and even leaves from the bushes outside littered the floor. Amin had been looking out the rear
window, at a view of another tenement building with
an old woman draping cloth over a wooden railing.
He turned and said to Gavril, who sat in one of the
chairs, "Why did you insist that I come here? You
know the kind of risk I'm taking."

"And what of the risks I've taken?" asked Gavril.
"I'm a hunted man, Amin. I'm here because of you.
Your cause. Your country."

"It is *our* cause," Amin corrected him. "We are
brothers in this, are we not?"

"Then I must be the poor brother, for you are the
one with the chalet on Lake Geneva and the num-
bered bank accounts."

"That money has been used to help you before,
Gavril, as it is being used now."

Gavril stood and moved to the window so that he
could see the other tenements, as if that would un-

derscore the poverty around them, bring greater force to his words. He said, "If it took only money, Amin, you wouldn't need me, would you? Jihar and his followers will die to free this country of Nahir. How much is their blood worth?"

"Perhaps that is what I should be asking you."

"We have already embarrassed Nahir's friends by stealing the arms shipment from these invincible Marines," Gavril said. "Jihar and his men are going to believe in themselves more and more, and when they see the blood of these Marines flow freely—as it will—then you will get stronger."

"And when will that happen?" Amin asked.

"It is happening as we speak. And these Marines will do nothing, just as they have done before. Just give me what I ask and soon enough Jemal will be in your hands. These Americans will be gone. They will soon abandon Nahir. You have my word, brother."

"I believe you, brother," Amin said.

Outside, they could hear a car's engine reverberating against the smooth stone. Gavril looked down, watched as a man got out of the back and assisted a woman with mirrored sunglasses from the back. The man helped Elli Bauman into the building, using a door that was nearly directly under him.

Gavril turned and said, "If you will excuse me, I have to meet with someone." He walked to the door, opened it, and then stopped for a moment. "Your escort will return shortly. Please be patient."

Bauman was taken to a small, dirty room on the ground floor. Her guard touched her shoulder, telling her that she could sit down, helping her into the only chair in the room. He removed her sunglasses and then picked at the corner of the tape that held the gauze over her eyes. He peeled it free, tossed it on the floor, did the same with the bandage over the other eye, and then stood back, watching her. She raised her hands to her eyes and rubbed them briefly. She opened them, blinked rapidly, held up a hand to shield them, and then searched for her camera bag. It was on the floor near the door, waiting for her.

The guard stepped to the door, picked up the camera case, and gestured her out. She followed him up the flimsy stairs and waited while he set the case on a table. She rummaged through it, got out her Nikon 35mm, checked to make sure that there was film in it, and then stepped into the hallway. A man waved her forward and as she moved along the hall, she was joined by Jihar. She didn't speak to him, just waited as he opened a door for her.

She entered a darkened room. The two Marines sat in chairs in front of her, the flag of the rebels tacked to the wall behind them. Flanking the Marines were four hooded rebels. Bauman knew what was wanted. She raised her camera, took a picture, moved to the right and took three more. She changed the settings on the camera lens, grimaced at the lighting, and finished off the roll of film.

Jihar then stepped close to one of the hooded men and mumbled to him. The man nodded and turned, grabbing Ramirez, forcing him to stand. Two of the other hooded men jerked Halloran to his feet and pushed him to a side door.

When the Marines and the rebels were gone, Bauman turned to Gavril, the only man remaining. Maude Wynter stood next to him. Bauman looked from one to the other and then said, "I resent being used like this, Gavril."

"I thought you were sympathetic to our cause," Gavril said quietly.

"Maybe your cause, but not your methods."

Gavril shook his head slightly and said, "You idealists are all the same, Miss Bauman. You talk change and revolution but you're not willing to pay the price for it."

"Why should the Americans listen to me?" she asked him pointedly.

"You're a journalist. A neutral person. Cooperate, Miss Bauman, if you want those men to live. Cooperate." Gavril studied her for a moment and then moved to the door, opened it, and followed Jihar and the others.

Bauman and Wynter were left alone. Bauman stepped to the door she had used, opened it, and walked down the hallway to where she had left her camera bag. She put her camera in it and turned to find Wynter staring at her.

"Why is it you look so familiar to me?" Wynter asked her suspiciously.

Bauman closed her case, snapped the catches, and turned. She looked at Wynter and shrugged. She didn't want to speak to Wynter. She just wanted to get out of the dirty tenement and away from the terrorists.

"We've met before," Wynter told her.

"Where?"

Wynter smiled. "Amsterdam," she said as if revealing classified information.

"You were with a group of students who came to visit Hans," she said cautiously.

"That's right," Wynter said. "You were with Hans Kroger. You were friends."

"We were more than friends," Bauman said quietly, almost stiffly.

"It must have been very painful for you," said Wynter, her voice conveying not sympathy, but sarcasm.

"I still miss Hans, and I still hate the Zionist bastards who killed him, if that's what you want to know," Bauman said sharply.

"I didn't mean to upset you."

"You haven't upset me. It's just a very sensitive subject. I guess I'm not over it yet."

"Death is a selfish lover."

"Are you comfortable with it?" Bauman asked.

"When you're as close to death as I have been, you learn to embrace it."

"Somehow I can't get used to that idea," Bauman said, moving to the window.

Wynter smiled. "The closer you get to it, the easier it is," she said.

Bauman heard something below her and looked out the window. In the alley below she could see two guards standing on either side of the door leading into the tenement. She saw them turn to the left, toward the sound of a fruit peddler shouting to all, "I have oranges, beautiful oranges. Sweet melons and pomegranates."

As Bauman watched, the pushcart entered the alley. One of the guards moved toward it and as the peddler stopped, the guard reached down to grab an orange. He held it up, showing it to the other guard, who approached, smiling. Both of them inspected the fruit, pawing through it and holding up an orange or pomegranate or melon, and then replacing it. The peddler hovered around them, returning their smiles. He held up a melon and thumped the surface of it, listening to it, to prove that it was ripe. He hefted it, holding it beside his face, displaying it for the guards. Neither of them noticed the gold wings ripped from Halloran's uniform lying in the dirt near one of the cart's wheels.

Bauman finally turned away from the window. She stepped to the table and picked up her camera bag, slipping the strap over her shoulder. She looked at Wynter, didn't want to speak to the woman again, but felt she had to say something. "I had better get back to the hotel and get the pictures developed."

Bauman sat in one of the high-backed wingchairs in front of the ambassador's desk. She was still wearing a khaki skirt, shirt, and a bush jacket, complete with bullet loops for the big rounds needed to knock down elephants. She had put the mirrored sunglasses in her pocket. She had left her camera bag at the hotel, but did have a big purse with a small camera in it.

The ambassador sat behind his desk. He had studied the woman when she had entered, had called Sergeant Burns to join them, and waited while Burns slipped into the other chair. He pushed an envelope of pictures to the corner of his desk, waited while Burns flipped through them and set them back. The ambassador rubbed his face as if tired, looked at Bauman and said, "Reality is, Ms. Bauman, the United States does not and will not negotiate with terrorists."

Bauman watched Burns for a moment and then turned to the ambassador. "I know that, Mr. Ambassador, and I don't appreciate being used as a messenger by such people."

"Then why are you here?" Burns asked.

She snapped her head around to stare at Burns. "Look, if I can help in any way for you to get your people back, then I'm willing to do that."

Burns rolled his eyes and stared at the ceiling. "Why don't I believe you?"

The ambassador interrupted. "If you have any influence at all with these people that are holding our men—"

"I have no influence," she said. "I'm a conduit to the media for them and that's all."

"That's a crock of shit!" barked Burns. "Why are you always around when something is going down?"

"That's my job," she shot back.

"Is it your job watching innocent people being killed?" Burns snarled.

"Let's calm down, Sergeant," said the ambassador. "This tact isn't getting us anywhere."

"You're damned right it's not!" Burns said, slamming a hand to the arm of the chair. "Let's just throw her ass in prison with the other rebels, and—"

"All right, that's enough, Burns!" said the ambassador. He focused his attention on Burns but didn't speak to him again. Finally he looked at Bauman. "Miss Bauman, I will convey the rebel's demands to the State Department and when I get an official reply, you'll hear from us."

Bauman got to her feet, stooped to pick up her purse, and said, "I'll be at my hotel, Mr. Ambassador." She looked at Burns, but he kept his eyes on the corner of the desk where the pictures still sat. She turned and walked across the ornate rug and stepped onto the hardwood floor, the heels of her shoes tapping sharply.

As soon as she was gone, the ambassador said, quietly, "Sergeant Burns, I care about Colonel Hal-

loran and Sergeant Ramirez. I care a lot, but I have
to go by the book. The colonel knows that." He hesitated and then added, "It comes with the job."

Burns put his hands on his knees and pushed himself up out of the chair. "Well, Mr. Morgan, all I can
say is, it's a lousy job." He turned and walked from
the room, stopping long enough to close the door.

Outside he saw James waiting for him. He glanced
at the corporal, and continued down the hall, toward
his office. "What's up, Corporal?"

James fell in beside him and said, "There's this
old Arab dude who insists on talking to you,
Gunny."

Burns stopped at the door to his office and opened
it. "What about?"

James shrugged. "He won't say nothing, but he
had these on him when we searched him.

Burns looked down and saw a battered and dirty
set of gold wings.

CHAPTER SIX

The man in the expensive, dark blue, three-piece suit sat by himself at a small table in a room furnished with only a table, two chairs, and a single, overhead fan. The walls had been recently painted a light blue and the tile on the floor was worn but clean. There was a window on one wall that looked out onto the courtyard below, but the man in the suit couldn't see the ground. He could only see the face of the building across the way, a dung-colored structure with black bars on the windows and guards patrolling on top.

The door opened and two men entered. One of them was a prison guard wearing a sidearm and carrying a clipboard. The other was Hamed. The guard set the clipboard on the table, watched as the man scribbled a signature on it with a silver pen he had taken from the inside pocket of his suit. Without a word, he picked up the clipboard, stared at Hamed for a moment, and then left.

The man picked up his briefcase, opened the door, and gestured to the hallway, ignoring the guard who had been satisfied with the signature. "Your friends are waiting for you outside," he said.

They walked down a hallway, pushed the button

for the elevator, and waited. There was a window at the end of a short hall to the left and a potted palm near the elevator. The dirt in the pot was littered with paper and cigarette butts.

Hamed stared nervously at the numbers above the elevator door, wishing that it would hurry. He was afraid that someone would rush out of somewhere and tell him it was all a mistake. That he would have to return to the tiny, wet cell, to wait for the American to come to question him again. To listen to the screams of the other prisoners from deep in the building.

And then the elevator was there. The doors opened and Hamed was so relieved to discover the elevator was empty that he nearly leaped into it. He watched the man with the briefcase push the button, felt the floor drop from under him and then slow as the elevator stopped on the first floor.

At the main entrance, they stopped again. The man opened his briefcase to show the interior of it to the guard behind a panel of bulletproof glass. He checked a list on his desk, and then nodded, pushing a button hidden under the edge of his desk.

There was a loud, annoying buzz as the main door popped open. The man shut his briefcase, snapped the catches, and pushed on the door. He gestured Hamed out into the bright light of the late afternoon.

Across the street a car waited. The man with the briefcase led Hamed to it and opened the front door opposite the driver. Hamed ducked and got in. The man shut the door and then looked in the window of the rear door. He threw a half salute to the two people in the back, a man and a woman, then turned and walked across the street to his own car.

Maude Wynter asked, "How did it go, Hamed? Were they hard on you?"

"They humiliated me," Hamed said, his voice quiet. He stared at the floor between his feet.

Jihar, the man in the back, leaned forward and asked, "The police?"

"No," Hamed said without turning his head. "The other prisoners. I told them I was a freedom fighter and they laughed. They humiliated me."

Wynter leaned forward and placed a hand on Hamed's shoulder. "Don't worry, Hamed. You'll get your opportunity to prove to them what a real man is." She glanced at Jihar and smiled as she massaged Hamed's shoulder.

Jack Burns was leaning on his desk, a rough sketch between his hands. Near it was a photocube filled with pictures of Dana, and beside that were in and out baskets filled with papers. A single black pen stenciled with U.S. GOVERNMENT was near his hand.

The only person in the room with him was the old Arab fruit peddler. He too was looking at the sketch he had just completed. He pointed and said, "Stair here. Here." His voice was quiet and his English barely understandable.

Burns moved around and sat down in his chair. He looked up at the old man, studying his face, wondering if he was for real, or if he was an agent. Then the question became an agent for whom. Everybody and his brother, or sister, had agents operating in Jemal. All the fruit peddler was really doing was telling him that Halloran and Ramirez had been abducted, and he already knew that. Of course, he was adding one fact: the possible location of the two missing men. The broken and tarnished wings were a flimsy piece of evidence, but it was the only clue they had.

"You've been inside?' Burns asked.

The old man nodded and gestured, his hands waving in the air. "Is my home... long time back. Before fighting." He nodded vigorously as if approving of what he had just said, as if to convince Burns that it was correct. "Building same. Same."

Burns watched the man a moment longer and then slapped the edge of his desk. The old man had to be telling him the truth. The old man might be a lot of things, but Burns didn't think an actor was among them. Finally he got to his feet, folded the map of the tenement, and escorted the old Arab to the door where Corporal James waited.

"Help our friend find his way out," Burns said.

James turned and gestured toward the elevator. "This way, please."

"See that he is rewarded for his assistance," Burns said. "I think he's helped us more than he knows."

While James and the Arab peddler waited for the elevator, Burns walked down the hallway to the ambassador's office. "Is he in?" he asked the secretary when she looked up from the papers on her desk.

"Just a moment," she said. She picked up the phone, pushed a button on it, and whispered into it. She cradled the phone quietly and said, "You may go in."

Burns nodded his thanks and opened the door. Without preamble, he spread out the map of the tenement on the ambassador's desk and set the gold wings next to it. Quickly he told Morgan the story and what he wanted to do, how he planned to get Colonel Halloran and Sergeant Ramirez away from the terrorists.

The ambassador studied the map like it held the secrets of the universe. He rubbed a hand through his graying hair and looked at Burns. "This Arab peddler, how do you know it's not a trap?"

"The rebels want a negotiation, not a confrontation," Burns said evenly.

"Exactly," said the ambassador. "That's why I'm not going to support this plan of yours." He reached over and picked up the receiver.

"Who are you calling?"

"The palace. The Jemalis should know about this," said the ambassador.

"Hang up, Mr. Morgan," Burns said. He couldn't believe that the ambassador would trust the lives of Halloran and Ramirez to the Jemalis. It was the same stupid arrangement they had had in Vietnam. Everything had to be coordinated through a Vietnamese liaison officer, who was usually connected to the VC, so that the enemy knew everything as it was planned. Burns was sure that the Jemali government was connected to the terrorists in the same fashion and that anything the Jemali government knew, the terrorists would know within an hour. "Think about it. What if there is a leak?" he asked.

Morgan slammed the phone down. He leaned forward on his desk and stared at Burns. "Dammit, Sergeant, there's got to be another way."

"There is no other way." He picked up the wings and examined them. The ambassador didn't understand that the wings symbolized more than just ten jumps out of an airplane. They symbolized a brotherhood. They symbolized a relationship that demanded support of one another. If one man got into trouble it was the duty of his fellows to get him out.

"We've got to get in there and hit them fast, get our people out."

"We're a diplomatic office," the ambassador reminded him, "not an assault force. I say no. We'll wait till we hear from the State Department."

"We've got to go in now before they move them," Burns said, trying to keep the anger out of his voice. He refused to look up at the ambassador. He kept his attention focused on the map the peddler had drawn.

"I want Halloran back in one piece," said the ambassador. "I won't risk his life on some reckless move that I'm not convinced is necessary."

"Unless the State Department says so, is that it?" Burns asked sarcastically.

"That's it."

Burns took the map from the ambassador's desk and folded it up. "I hope you don't have to tell that to Mrs. Halloran," he said.

Hamed sat in a rough wooden chair in the old tenement building. The second-floor room was nearly bare, the window showing a dark night sky and a pool of light from a single lamp on the building across the way. The rebel flag was attached to the wall behind him. He looked at Jihar, who sat calmly.

"It is your decision," said Jihar. "I will not deny you. Only . . ."

Hamed nodded gravely and said decisively, "Then I will do it."

There was a sound from the connecting room and Jihar looked toward it and then back at Hamed. "First, listen to me, Hamed. Then decide. Perhaps you underestimate your value to our organization."

There was a shout next door. Jihar recognized

Zabib's voice, but he couldn't understand what was being said. He knew that Zabib was taking his pathological hatred of foreigners out on the two Americans they had captured. For a moment he thought about cautioning Zabib: they didn't want the prisoners to accidentally die—at least, not yet. He returned his attention to Hamed.

"The others do not respect me!" Hamed said, his voice rising to a shout. "In the jail they did not *respect* me!"

"They will," Jihar said soothingly. "In time they will all respect you." He stood and moved to the door, looking into the room where the hostages were being guarded. Ramirez was being held upright by two big rebels who wore hoods. There were bruises on his face and he was bleeding from his mouth and nose. Sweat glistened on his face and his hair hung damply. His uniform was torn and stained with his sweat and blood. He was sagging in the grasp of the two rebels.

To the side, Jihar could see Maude Wynter watching intently, her lips slightly parted. She sat in an old wooden chair, leaning forward. When Zabib hit Ramirez in the stomach, she smiled, enjoying the beating. She shifted around slightly, to see better.

Zabib hit Ramirez again, as if to get his attention. "How many freedom frighters you are killing now, Marine?" he shouted. *"How many?"*

Jihar started to move back out of the doorway. He felt his shoulder touched and turned to see Gavril standing behind him. He nodded a greeting.

Gavril patted Jihar on the shoulder and stepped by him, into the hostage room. As he passed the big man, he took the doorknob, gestured Jihar into the room, then tugged it closed. He moved close to

Wynter and saw the glassy look on her face as she watched Zabib continue to hit the Marine, first in the face and then in the stomach.

Ramirez slumped forward, his chin on his chest, as if he had lost consciousness. Zabib lifted his chin to hit him again, and Ramirez opened his eyes, but the blank look remained on his face. He was dazed but conscious.

Gavril eased closer to Halloran, who was being held in a chair, forced to watch the beating. Gavril leaned close to him so that his lips were next to Halloran's ear and said reasonably, "What about it, Colonel? Sign this confession saying you brought arms here to suppress the people and save your sergeant a beating."

"Go fuck yourself," Halloran said evenly.

"The colonel is a hard man," Maude said. She kept her eyes locked on Ramirez, enjoying his pain, wishing that she could do something to increase it. Slowly she turned so that she could see a Black and Decker power drill lying on the table. There was an extralong bit in it. She got to her feet and moved to the table to pick it up, studying the point of the bit as if she had never seen anything so interesting.

"Made in America," Gavril said.

Wynter nodded at two terrorists. "Take his hand," she ordered, indicating Halloran.

One of them grabbed the back of the chair while the other tied Halloran's right hand to the side of the chair, out of the way. He stretched Halloran's left hand out on top of an old wooden table stained with blood from other victims. The first man moved around and leaned on Halloran's elbow so that the colonel could not move his arm or hand.

"Perhaps I can drill some sense into him," she said as she stared at him almost lovingly.

Halloran strained against the ropes that held him in the chair. He tightened the muscles of his right arm and pulled. He felt the rope bite deep, cutting into the skin. He filled his lungs with air and pushed against the ropes around his chest, but they didn't give at all. He felt sweat bead on his forehead and drip down his sides. He blinked his eyes rapidly because of the sweat splashing into them.

Wynter pulled the trigger on the drill and watched the tip of it spin. She grinned at it and then glanced at Halloran, smiling at him. She let go of the trigger and then pulled it, again and again, so that the sound of the drill filled the air. She let Halloran anticipate her next move for a moment, letting the fear build, waiting for Halloran to beg or plead for mercy, for him to prove that he was as weak as the others.

But Halloran didn't beg or plead. The only visible sign from the Marine colonel was his silent attempt to break the ropes with his muscles. He pulled and pushed, the ropes biting deep into his flesh, the blood welling from under them to mingle with his sweat and drip to the floor.

Wynter held the trigger of the drill down; the sound filled the room, drowning the rasp of Halloran's rapid breathing, and the smell of the oil on the heating electric motor overpowered the odor of sweat. Without warning, she whirled and shoved the bit into the back of Halloran's hand. It sliced through the skin easily, squirting blood, and then met the resistance of bone. There was the high-pitched sound of an electric drill fighting through a tough piece of wood, joined by the sound of Halloran's scream of pain, and then sudden silence as Halloran collapsed, moaning with pain and willing himself to stay conscious.

Wynter reversed the spin, pulled the trigger, and jerked the drill bit free. Blood spattered her face. She stared at the wound in Halloran's hand, blood flowing from it, and slowly licked her lips, tasting it. She grinned and handed the drill to Zabib.

"Now it's your turn, Sergeant," Gavril said.

The two men who had held Ramirez, forcing him to watch Wynter torture Halloran, gripped him tighter. A chair was shoved under his leg and a rebel rolled up the trouser leg to expose his knee. Ramirez looked at his bare knee, at Wynter, Halloran's blood smeared on her face, and then at the colonel. Halloran was slumped in his chair, his face wet with sweat. There were large stains under his arms and down his back. He carefully kept his eyes away from Halloran's left hand and the bloody hole that had been drilled in it.

Zabib moved closer and pulled the trigger on the drill, letting it spin, watching Ramirez. The terror was evident on his face. Halloran hadn't known exactly what was going to happen, but Ramirez knew. He knew that they were about to cripple him. He could almost feel the point of the drill biting into his flesh, pressing through the cartilage and bone and tissue. He could almost see the blood pouring from his knee, almost hear his own screams of anguish.

Zabib lowered the drill slowly until the point was a fraction of an inch from Ramirez's knee cap. Ramirez thought he could feel it spinning, feel the heat from the bit as it spun above his skin.

"Oh no!" he pleaded. "No! *No!* Please! Lemme make a statement or something. I'll sign papers." He tore his eyes away from his knee and choked back a sob, but then seemed to break down. "Don't fuck me up, man. I'll do anything . . ."

Zabib grinned sadistically and began to press the drill down so that it just touched the skin on Ramirez's knee, scratching it, drawing a little blood.

"Wait!" Gavril ordered. Calmly, he took a cigarette from the pack in his pocket and lit it. He tossed the match to the floor and walked toward Zabib. He looked at Halloran, who watched the scene but hadn't said a word yet. Halloran looked disgusted by the breakdown of a fellow Marine.

Gavril put a restraining hand on Zabib, taking the Black and Decker drill from him with the other. He turned and smiled at Ramirez. He motioned to the rebels holding Ramirez's leg to release it.

"Will you have these same sentiments in the morning, Sergeant?" he asked. He smiled at the Marine sergeant, radiating kindness.

"Sergeant Ramirez!" Halloran snapped, his voice furred with pain. "Don't forget who you are."

For a moment Ramirez said nothing. He looked at Halloran and then at his hand on the table, a pool of blood around it. His eyes searched out Halloran's, but when they met, Ramirez looked away, ashamed. For a moment he stared at a spot on the floor and then turned his attention to Gavril, looking at him as if Gavril were his savior. A man who could do anything, and would do anything to help him. Ramirez nodded almost imperceptibly, acknowledging his defeat.

"I'll do anything you want," Ramirez mumbled. He spoke quietly as if he could keep Halloran from hearing him. As if he could keep Halloran from knowing that he was betraying him. He only wanted Gavril and the others to hear his words. "Just don't put that thing in my leg." He stared at Gavril, his eyes fixed on the cigarette that he was smoking.

Gavril noticed that. He took the cigarette from his mouth, exhaling a giant cloud of blue smoke. Seeming to inspect the cigarette, he gently asked, "Would you like a cigarette, Sergeant?"

Ramirez swallowed hard, as if the act were painful. He took a deep breath. He smiled weakly and then nodded. "I'm dyin' for a cigarette."

Gavril glanced around, set the drill on the vacant chair, and fished a cigarette out of the pack. He lit it, tossed away the match, and put the cigarette between Ramirez's lips.

Ramirez inhaled gratefully, sucking the smoke deep into his lungs. He leaned back slightly and closed his eyes. He tried to smile his thanks, but started coughing violently, the cigarette flying from his mouth. He bent at the waist, trying to stop.

Disgusted, Gavril waved to the men holding Ramirez, telling them to let him go. Ramirez continued to cough, his free arms wrapped around his waist as if trying to hold himself together. He bent forward so that his face was nearly to his knees and he was looking at the floor.

Zabib watched the display, sneering. He glanced at the other rebels and then back at Ramirez. "Is our cigarette too strong for the American Marine?" he asked mockingly. He laughed and took a pack of Marlboros from his own pocket, shaking a single cigarette from it. He held the cigarette out like a piece of candy offered as a reward.

Ramirez had straightened up, the fit of coughing over. With a trembling hand, he reached out for the cigarette, his eyes locked on those of Zabib. Without looking, he reached out with his other hand and snatched the drill from the chair. Before anyone could react, Ramirez slammed it into Zabib's chest, pulling the trigger and jamming it forward with all his might, driving Zabib back.

"Pendejo mother-fucker!" he snarled, leaning his weight into the drill, trying to push it through Zabib. Blood spattered his face and chest.

Zabib staggered backward and then fell, control gone from his legs. He reached for the drill, but when his hand touched it, the pain froze him. He screamed then, his hands around the drill, holding it up so that it wouldn't hurt him anymore. He could feel the spreading warmth of blood as it drained from his body and stained his shirt. It slid down his sides and began pooling under him.

Ramirez spun as Zabib fell, grabbing at Gavril's gun, but one of the terrorists leaped forward, stopping him. Ramirez hit the man in the side of the head, spinning him out of the way. He clubbed him with his fist, crushing him to the floor. Before he could move again, another of the rebels came at him. Ramirez feinted and punched, then kicked upward. As his foot connected, a third rebel grabbed him from behind, holding him. Ramirez bucked wildly, trying to shake free, trying to get leverage so that he could throw the man, but it was already too late. Two more terrorists came at him, grabbing him and holding him so that he couldn't move.

Jihar, who had been standing out of the way, watching, shouldered his way past the other rebels. To his left, Zabib lay, his shirt covered with bright red blood. One man held his head, trying to comfort Zabib, who was dying. His face had taken on a waxy look, the blood already draining from it. Zabib's eyes were unfocused and staring, as if looking at something a hundred feet above him. Jihar turned so that he was face-to-face with Ramirez. He stared at Ramirez, waiting for him to do something, but Ramirez couldn't move with the terrorists holding him.

"Well, come on, shithead," demanded Ramirez. He glared at Jihar, daring him. "What the fuck you waiting for? Gimme your best shot."

Jihar seemed to swell. He ducked his head slightly and took a swing at Ramirez, hitting him in the mouth, smashing his lips and loosening his teeth. Jihar drew his fist back and a roar bubbled in his throat, erupting into a scream of animal rage. One of the terrorists tried to restrain him, but Jihar shook himself free, sending the man sprawling. He reached out, both arms extended as if he were going to hug a friend. He seized Ramirez, shaking him so that the rebels holding him released him. Jihar lifted Ramirez from his feet as he bent back slightly. He locked his hands behind Ramirez's back and began to squeeze, roaring at the top of his voice, an animal lost in blood lust, unaware of the others around him, cheering him on, shouting for him to squash the Marine. Jihar leaned his face against Ramirez's chest, squeezing, his muscles knotting. Sweat popped onto his forehead with the exertion.

Halloran jerked at his ropes, trying to free himself so he could help Ramirez but every little movement sent slivers of pain through his wounded hand and up into his arm. He gritted his teeth, trying one last time, the cords knotting on his neck, the muscles rippling in his right arm and chest, but it did no good. The ropes were too strong and tied too tight. He was helpless. He could do nothing for Ramirez.

Jihar was still squeezing Ramirez, who was nearly

unconscious. At first Ramirez had tried to free his arms to fight back, but Jihar held him too tightly. Jihar jerked him up and down and could feel the bones of Ramirez's spine popping and cracking under the strain.

Ramirez's face changed to a bright red as he tried to breathe but no longer had the strength. He felt himself grow hot and he kicked with his feet, but missed everything. He tried it again, but now the motions were too weak. The blows bounced harmlessly off the giant Arab. He saw a curtain of black lowering over his eyes and knew that he was on the verge of passing out. He struggled harder, trying to free himself, but felt his will, his life, slipping away from him.

Jihar felt the tension leave Ramirez. His head was lolling, swinging with each motion Jihar made, but Jihar didn't release the pressure, he increased it, squeezing tighter and tighter until he was sure that the Marine was dead. Then he dropped to one knee, Ramirez's body across the other. Jihar put one massive forearm across the top of Ramirez's chest and the other over his hips and jerked downward. He felt Ramirez's spine snap under the strain and knew that if the Marine hadn't been dead before, he was now. He rolled the body to the floor and spit on its back. Without a word to anyone in the room, he left.

CHAPTER SEVEN

Corporal Ruggieri sat watching the bank of TV monitors, bored by the afternoon duty that rarely provided anything more exciting than one of the embassy limousines sliding through the front gate. He glanced up at the wall clock above the monitors, as the minute hand snapped to the twelve with an audible click and realized that his shift was nearly over. He flicked his attention from one screen to the next, looking at an empty corridor, an almost deserted foyer where he could only see the gleaming shoes of another of the Marine guards, and then looked at one that showed the street approach to the embassy.

At the top of that screen, an old van with a dented front and cracked windshield appeared. It was speeding toward the gate, almost as if it were going to crash through it. Using one of the joystick controls, Ruggieri changed the angle on the camera so that he could see the van better. As the camera panned upward, he caught a glimpse of the Jemali guard peering out of his booth near the gate, holding his rifle in both hands, unsure of what to do with it.

Ruggieri turned his attention back to the van, which had slowed as it came abreast with the embassy gate. The rear doors flew open and Ruggieri could see two men dressed in khaki uniforms and wearing kaffiyeh to obscure their faces holding some kind of large bundle between them. They rolled it off the back and were reaching out to slam the doors when Ruggieri realized they had tossed a body from the van. He refused to recognize the blue trousers and khaki shirt of the embassy's Marine security force.

His eyes glued to the screen, he reached with his left hand for the receiver of the phone that tied him to Sergeant Burns in the security office. He punched the button beside the phone, heard a buzz at the other end, and then a voice growled, "Burns."

Quickly he explained what he had seen on the monitor and then said, "He was dumped in the street! I think it's Sergeant Ramirez, Gunny!"

Burns slammed his phone down and ran from the room. The elevator doors were open as he stepped into the hallway. He shouted at the man who was getting on, telling him to hold it as he rushed forward. On the ground level, he ran down the corridor to the front door, waited while the Marine guard there buzzed him through the door.

Outside he could see a crowd starting to gather a short distance from the body, obviously a Marine. Some of them were Jemalis who were walking by, some of them guards at the embassy, both Marine and Jemali, and the rest were men and women of the embassy staff. He could see the body lying in the street. There was a noise behind him, a sound between a growl and shout of rage, and he saw James running across the compound. He slowed at the gate, burst through it and slid to a stop near the body. He dropped to one knee and reached out with a hand as if to touch it, to find out if it was real.

Burns pushed his way through the crowd and stood for a moment looking down at the battered body, the uniform torn and stained. James had turned him over, identified him as Ramirez, and was cradling his head in his arms. Burns bent over, gently pushed James aside and picked up Ramirez. As he lifted the body from the street, the tiny flag that Ramirez had been so proud of fell from his pocket. Burns didn't see it drop.

As Burns moved through the crowd again, James reached down and picked up the flag. He dusted it off, turned it over to look at the bottom, and then shoved it into his own pocket before moving back into the embassy.

Burns, his jaw set in a grim line, carried Ramirez into the embassy grounds, up to the main door, and through it. His first thought was to take Ramirez up to the ambassador's office and show him what waiting for the State Department to decide meant. Then he thought better of it and took Ramirez to the tiny dispensary that had been erected to treat embassy personnel's minor wounds and sicknesses.

The flag-draped coffin of Sergeant Ramirez sat on the tarmac behind the camouflaged United States Air Force C-130. An honor guard of Marines, each in dress uniform, stood at attention to one side of the coffin, their rifles held at present arms. Burns stood near them, a light, evening breeze tugging at his dress blue trousers as the sound of the aircraft's engines tried to drown out every other noise.

Standing just off the tarmac, behind a short, chain-link fence was a group of embassy men and women. They were a grim, sad-faced group with several of the women crying softly as they stared into the dusk.

Burns did an about-face, and ordered, "Detail. Ready."

The seven Marines in the line near the coffin came to port arms, their faces set, grim, staring at the distant horizon. Their white caps were pulled low over their heads, so it was hard to see their faces.

"Aim."

The Marines snapped their rifles to their shoulders in a single, fluid motion, and aimed upward at a forty-five-degree angle.

"Fire!"

There was a single, sharp report as if only one weapon had fired. As soon as they had pulled the triggers, Burns ordered them to fire again; then a third time, a slight hesitation between each round. When the last of the echoes from the third volley died away, Burns said, "Order, arms."

Then, as a Marine bugler blew the first note of "Taps," Burns ordered the detail to "Present arms." He turned toward the coffin, came to attention, and saluted, as the bugler continued with the haunting melody.

James was standing at attention, saluting, his gaze fixed on the coffin, the American flag rippling gently in the breeze. He was biting his lip, trying to hold back his grief. His left hand was pressed against his thigh with enough pressure to cause him some pain. He kept his eyes averted, as if he could deny the existence of the coffin by ignoring it.

Next to him, Ruggieri was crying openly, the tears staining his cheeks as he saluted the coffin. Unlike James, he couldn't look away. Irrationally, he hoped that Ramirez would suddenly lift the coffin's lid and climb out, laughing at the great joke he had played on everyone.

Burns hadn't moved except to snap his right hand to the bill of his cap. He stood at rigid attention, his face a mask of grim determination. His eyes were on the embassy people across the tarmac. He could see a couple of women crying, handkerchiefs to their eyes. One man wiped his hand across his eyes as if to brush away tears there.

Burns was surprised by the display of emotion. Other than the Marines standing near him, none of the people actually knew Ramirez, and he would be surprised to learn that any of them had ever spoken to him. Maybe it was because it was a fellow American, cut down by terrorists, and each of the people realized that it could easily have been him or her. Or maybe it was a reminder that death lurked near them all. Whatever it was, the people were genuinely affected by the small ceremony and by Ramirez's death.

"Taps" ended but the notes seemed to hang in the air momentarily. Eight Marines moved from a position at the rear of the formation and went forward to pick up the coffin. Two of them moved to the ends and picked up the American flag, folding it quickly and expertly until it was a small blue triangle covered with white stars. When they had finished, they stepped to the rear as the remaining six picked up the coffin, and then moved forward slowly, each step measured. With great precision they carried Ramirez to the rear ramp of the C-130. They slid the coffin inside the cargo plane and then stepped back, out of the way. Slowly, the ramp rose until the men on the tarmac could no longer see the coffin.

The Marine with the flag carried it to Burns, who dropped his salute and took it. He then spun to face the rest of the detail and yelled over the sound of the aircraft's engines, "Order arms." His voice cracked as he shouted the order, but he didn't think that anyone noticed.

As he moved to the side, away from the plane, the ambassador caught him and whispered to him, "I'm sorry, Sergeant, but this doesn't change anything."

Burns looked at the assembled honor guard. At the Marines holding their M16s and staring into the night. At the color guard, the four Marines, one of them holding the American flag, one of them holding the Marine colors filled with battle streamers from the Revolutionary War to Vietnam, and the two men with their rifles, flanking them. At the Marines who had carried the coffin, and the others who had just been present to salute a fallen comrade.

"It does for me," he said.

An hour later, Burns was in the arms locker in the embassy. He had changed from the dress uniform that he had worn during the ceremony at the airport. He was now wearing camouflaged fatigues, jump boots, and crossed bandoliers of cloth ammo pouches. He wiped the sweat from his face with the back of his sleeve as he reached for another weapon. There were weapons designed for every contingency stored there. Riot guns, Remington shotguns with grenade launchers under the barrel, revolvers, both regular .38s and .357s, M16s, Uzi submachine guns, and even a couple of old .45 caliber automatics. As Burns reached out to grab one of the Uzis, he revealed a tattoo on his forearm: DEATH BEFORE DISHONOR.

Burns grabbed one of the Remington shotguns and handed it to James, who backed out of the locker. Ruggieri stood next to him, holding an Uzi and a shotgun. Burns straightened up and closed the door to the locker. He turned and moved down the hallway and entered his office, Ruggieri and James right behind him.

In his office, he set one of the shotguns on his desk and unfolded the map the fruit peddler had given him. The three men crowded around it and studied it again, searching for details they might have missed. Burns then opened the top drawer of his desk and pulled out a stick of camouflage paint. He smeared some of it on the back of his hand. He then turned James around and began covering his face with the stuff.

Ruggieri took another stick of paint, a darker color, and started putting it on his own face. When he had finished, he handed it to Burns, who used it to disguise the highlights on James's cheekbones, chin, and forehead. It was meant to keep light from reflecting from the skin at night, rather than to help conceal them during the day.

It was after midnight when Burns led them from the security office, down the elevator, and outside. They climbed into a jeep and Burns started the engine. They drove off the embassy grounds, turned onto the wide street lined with other embassies and governmental offices, and began a slow journey through the city, being careful not to arouse suspicion. They drove past shops with their bright-colored awnings, old buildings with faded signs and shuttered windows, past people who huddled in doorways or crouched under stairways. They used narrow streets that looped back and forth, and wide avenues that ran straight. They passed traffic circles with fountains in the center of them and large squares of green dotted with colored flowers, built to prove that Jemal was not an arid wasteland.

Burns never deviated from a direct course because he was certain that he knew where Halloran was being held. Certain that the old fruit peddler had told them the truth. By morning, he hoped to have the problem resolved.

The sky to the east brightened from a deep black to a light gray tinged with pink. The tops of buildings became black shapes silhouetted against the lighter graying sky. The features of the tenement building were becoming more clearly defined as the sun came up. The windows were shuttered or boarded up to keep those outside from seeing what was happening inside. A single lamp threw a pool of light into the alleyway but it was being washed out by the rising sun.

Inside the main tenement building, an armed rebel guard sat at a table, flipping through a magazine. A small lamp sat on the table so that the guard could see the pictures. There was nothing else in the room except the prisoner.

Halloran was asleep in a chair four feet from the guard. His hands were bound behind him and his ankles were roped together with the rope looped through the rungs of the chair. He stirred slightly, opened his eyes, and saw the guard glance at him before returning to the magazine.

A door opposite Halloran opened and another rebel entered. Through the open door the terrorist could see more people asleep on mats on the floor. One man, just awakened, sat up and rubbed his bearded face. He mumbled something unintelligible to the man who had opened the door and then sank back to his mattress.

As the man lay back, Maude Wynter sat up, the thin sheet over her falling away, revealing her bare skin to the waist. She brushed her blond hair from her face, pushed it back over the top of her head, and looked to the right. She leaned over and gently shook Gavril's shoulder until he opened his eyes and sat up.

He looked at Wynter, smiled at her, and then glanced through the door where he could see still more of the rebels waking. One of them, wearing khaki-colored shorts, stood and stretched, his arms over his head. He turned to the left and looked at the balcony that overlooked the street. He could see a guard sitting there, staring to the east, waiting for the sun.

Another guard, unseen by Gavril, sat halfway down the stairs that led to the outside. That man had leaned to the side, letting his head rest against the wall. He was fighting off sleep, his half-closed eyes on the street. He saw one of the guards who roamed the outside pass the door, thought about waving to him, but didn't have the energy. He leaned his rifle against the wall because it suddenly seemed too heavy to hold.

A roving guard stopped near the corner of the building, glanced at his watch, then at the sky, and finally stretched. He shuddered in the early morning chill, the humid air coating everything with a fine layer of mist that was somehow sticky and irritating. He saw another of the guards sitting in the car parked next to a large bush away from the light, his chin against his chest, fast asleep. The rover moved toward him and tapped on the window opposite the sleeping man. He stooped to look, tapped on the window again, but got no response. In a harsh whisper, he said, "Wake up! They will be coming to relieve us soon."

Worried, he straightened and walked around the car, avoiding the bush. He reached down, tried to open the car door, and looked in the window again, realizing that something was wrong. The front of the guard's uniform was wet, stained with a dark ragged smear, but it was impossible to discern the color. Suddenly frightened, he looked closer at the man in the car, saw a wound at his throat, a tattered rip in the soft flesh of the neck, a wet wound that had to be fatal.

He took a step backward and was grabbed from behind. He lost his footing as someone kicked his feet out from under and he fell to his back. He stared upward, and could see a human shape above him holding a long knife in one hand, the blade glowing orange in the light of the rising sun.

The man with the knife, Corporal James, put his knee in the middle of the man's chest. He leaned forward, a hand over the mouth and nose of the guard to keep him from crying out. He felt the guard's teeth biting at his hand and used his knife. He felt it slice through the tender flesh of the throat with a quiet sound like silk being ripped. There was a splash of blood, covering James's hand and staining his uniform. The guard bucked once, as if trying to throw James, spasmed, and died.

James dragged the dead man deeper into the bush, hiding him. He then poked his head out and looked to the rooftop across the street, where he could barely see the shape of another man. James held out one hand, the thumb turned up.

Across the street, Burns saw the signal and returned it. He then looked at Ruggieri, who was across the roof crouched beside a skylight, occasionally looking down at the balcony where a sleepy guard waited for someone to bring him coffee or for his relief to show up. Ruggieri saw the signal, flashed one back at Burns, and waited for the explosion that would mark the beginning of the assault.

As Burns flipped another thumbs-up at James, James moved past the body of the dead guard, breathed deeply as if to calm himself, and looked across the open ground to the rear door of the tenement. He aimed his grenade launcher, felt for the safety, and flipped it off. He pulled the trigger and there was a quiet *pop* as the grenade fired. A second later there was a louder, brighter one as the door there exploded. James sprinted across the courtyard to the smoking ruins of the door, hit the wall with his back. He broke open the grenade launcher, jammed another round in it, and then glanced through the smoke and broken bits of the door.

On the stairs he saw another guard scrambling up, but not making much progress. He would slip, try to get to his feet and run, only to fall again. James poked the barrel of the grenade launcher around the corner, aimed it up at a forty-five-degree angle, and pulled the trigger.

The door at the top of the stairs blew up in a flash of light that threw wood splinters along the hall behind it and down the stairs in front of it like shrapnel from a mortar round. Part of the roof went up in the explosion, opening a hole, the debris cascading down. The guard took part of the explosion in the chest and somersaulted down the stairs to land sprawled half out the door at James's feet. Part of his face was missing and blood covered his chest.

As the first door blew, Burns was on his feet, sprinting across the roof. When the second one blew out part of the roof, he halted, looked through the opening, and then dropped through it. He was facing the street side and could see where boards had been nailed across the door to hide the room from the outside and the balcony. He opened fire with his Uzi, the thin wood of the boards shattering. The guard there had stood up with the first explosion outside and the bullets from Burns's weapon caught him in the chest and blew out his back. The man toppled over the railing and fell to the street.

Burns spun then, firing as he did, hosing down one of the sleeping rooms of the terrorists. He didn't aim his weapon, just pulled the trigger, firing from the hip, the slugs slamming into the men in the room, the furniture, the cots, the walls. The bolt of the weapon locked back and Burns tossed it aside, grabbing for a pump shotgun.

Outside, Ruggieri dropped from the rooftop to the balcony that Burns had just blasted clean. He dived through the shattered wood of the planking that had been over part of the door, and came up firing into the smoke-filled room. Through an open door, he could see one of the terrorists with a knife moving, but then the rebel who had been reading the magazine leaped forward, out of the shadows. Ruggieri spun, and fired a quick three-shot burst. The rebel took it high in the chest, flipping back against the wall, leaving a streak of red as he collapsed to the floor.

As he turned his attention to the door, one of the terrorists kicked at it, slamming it behind him as he fled. Ruggieri opened fire on it, riddling it with the 9mm slugs. When the bolt locked open, Ruggieri hit the release, dropped the magazine to the floor and slammed a fresh one home. He rushed across the room and hit the wall, his eyes on the bullet-damaged door.

At the foot of the stairs, James checked the body of the terrorist who had fallen there. The man was dead. James grabbed the man's knife, put it on the floor under his foot and lifted, snapping the blade so that it would be of no use to anyone who might find it. He took the man's pistol, stuck it inside his pistol belt, ripped the spare ammo from the dead man's uniform, and then started climbing the stairs, his weapon pointed at the door that he had blasted with his grenade.

He stopped at the top of the stairs, concealed by the debris, searching the smoke- and dust-filled hall, looking for either Burns or Ruggieri, or more of the rebels. He could hear firing nearby, in some of the rooms, but could see no one, other than a dead man lying against the wall, his blood pooling under his smashed head.

There was a sustained burst of fire that was punctuated by two shotgun blasts. James ran down the hallway, leaped over a broken chair, and glanced through the doorway.

Inside, Burns used the butt of his shotgun. He snapped it around sharply, upward, catching one of the terrorists under the chin, flipping him back. As that man hit the floor spurting blood and spitting teeth, Burns dropped to one knee and fired at the two remaining rebels. One of them was aiming a pistol at Ruggieri, who had just dived through another door. Burns fired at the terrorist, the blast catching the man head high. The body dropped, an explosion of crimson from the neck, where the head used to be. The last man dropped his weapon and tried to leap through the window, but Burns cut him down. The body hung across the sill, halfway out of the room, the blood running down the wall to stain the floor.

Burns surveyed the room, but all the rebels in it were either dead or dying. They were lying among the furniture, draped over one another, and sprawled near the door, their blood covering the floor.

Burns wanted to pick up the weapons, to keep them out of the hands of the terrorists still alive elsewhere in the building, but didn't have the men to do it. He would have to leave them for the moment. Later he would get a detail from the embassy to gather up the weapons, ammo, explosives, and any documents that might tell him something about the terrorist organization in Jemal.

Ruggieri jumped across the room to a door that was closed, and reached out as if to twist the knob. Burns saw James enter with his grenade launcher and waved Ruggieri away from the door. James loaded a grenade, pointed it at the door, and as he fired, Burns yelled, *"Now!"*

The door blew up and in, shattered. Burns dived through the cloud of dust and smoke and fired as he slid across the floor. He could see a single terrorist trying to flee through another door. The man took the whole blast in the middle of the back. He was lifted from his feet and smashed into the wall. He stood for a moment as if nailed there, the blood blossoming on his back, and then toppled over, a ragged bloodstain on the wall.

Burns leaped to his feet and ran across the room. Through the door, he could see the shapes of two people as they disappeared in the dark. He fired once, the muzzle flash lighting the stairs like a strobe, but he saw no one there. He looked back at the rebel, to make sure that the man was dead. To one side he could see a chair that had a piece of rope tied to it, and knew that Halloran had been in that chair only moments earlier. Since he was gone now, it meant that the colonel was still alive, because if he weren't, the terrorists would have left the body.

Still tacked to the wall was the rebel flag. There were a couple of bullet holes in it and a splatter of blood across the center of it. Burns stepped to it, ripped it from the wall, wadding it up. He tossed it on the floor and ground his heel into it contemptuously. Ruggieri and James joined him, standing on either side of the door, waiting for Burns to make the first move.

Burns started down the stairs, his back against the wall, his shotgun pointed low. He could hear the rebels in the dark below him, throwing things around, as if in a panic and trying to escape. He heard no voices until one of them shouted something in Arabic and the noise vanished.

Suddenly, there was a burst of fire from somewhere below. Burns could see the muzzle flashes in the dim light coming from the cellar. He jumped back as the bullets ripped into the wall near him. He scrambled back up the stairs, following James and Ruggieri. For a moment they stared at him. Burns smiled and jerked one of the hand grenades from his pistol belt. He pulled the pin and tossed it away. He put a finger to his lips as if telling them to be quiet and then threw the grenade, underhanded, down the stairs. They could hear it bounce on the steps, once, twice and on the third time it exploded. A second later the dust and smoke from the detonation boiled up and out.

In the tunnel, the fleeing rebels heard the firing behind them as one of the terrorists tried to cover their retreat. They heard his defense end in the explosion of the grenade, but now they were deep in the tunnel, running through it, scattering the rats that lived in the dim light there. A tunnel dug from the basement, braced with thick beams, lined with stone, and designed as an escape hatch in case their tenement was raided.

Jihar was carrying Halloran over his shoulder. The Marine colonel had his hands bound behind him, his wounded left hand in a rough, blood-soaked bandage.

As they continued along the tunnel, Jihar stumbled, catching his foot on something unseen in the dirt of the floor. He fell forward to his knees and let Halloran's feet touch the ground briefly.

Halloran didn't hesitate. He brought his knee up, catching Jihar under the jaw. The blow wasn't well placed, a stunning kick that dropped Jihar to his hands and knees but that left him conscious. Halloran didn't wait. He started running back the way they had come, his eyes on the rough stone walls of the tunnel. Far in front of him he could see a dim light, marking his goal.

Out of nowhere, Gavril and Wynter appeared, blocking his path. Halloran slid to a halt as Wynter raised her Walther and pointed at Halloran's face. In that instant, he thought he was going to die, that she was going to shoot him because he was no longer worth all the trouble. Instead, she just grinned at him, her eyes locked on his.

He felt a hand on his shoulder and was spun around so that he faced Jihar. The big man drew back his fist and hit Halloran once in the jaw. Halloran saw an explosion of white as he fell back, unconscious as he hit the tunnel floor.

Jihar reached down, picked up Halloran again, throwing him over his shoulder. Without a word to either Gavril or Wynter, he turned and trotted down the tunnel. He reached a ramp that led upward. Jihar climbed it, slowing only slightly. At the top was a wooden door reinforced with metal. He banged on it with his free hand, waited, hit it again, and growled under his breath, demanding that the door be opened.

A second later there was a bright crack and then the door opened, the bright, early morning sunlight flooding in. The young boy who had been playing soccer in the street when Halloran and Ramirez had been brought in stood there grinning. Jihar moved to the back of the van, and waited for the boy to open the doors. Then he dumped Halloran in the back and saw the big Marine stir as if he was beginning to regain consciousness.

Jihar pulled a pistol from under his belt, checked the magazine, chambered a round, and handed it to the boy. "Shoot him if he tries to escape."

The boy looked at Jihar and then slipped off the safety. He held the pistol in two hands and pointed it at Halloran.

Jihar nodded his approval and then turned, running back into the tunnel to help Gavril and Wynter.

As soon as the grenade exploded, Burns started down the stairs again, taking them slowly, feeling his way along the wall. He reached the basement floor and found the body of the terrorist lying near the entrance to the passage. The body was missing an arm, and one side was riddled with shrapnel. It looked like the terrorist had tried to catch the grenade and failed. Burns grabbed the weapon the terrorist had lost, threw it into the shadows, and then jumped to the side of the tunnel.

He looked back and saw both Ruggieri and James. James was the last one down, covering their rear. Ruggieri hit the other side of the wall and glanced down the tunnel, but could see nothing in the dimly lighted passage.

As James crossed the basement floor to join them, Burns glanced down the tunnel and then entered it, jogging along one wall. There were large wooden beams spaced along it and an occasional light that did little to dispel the gloom. Ruggieri and James were still behind him, James watching their rear.

A burst of fire hit the wall and beams near Burns, spattering him with dirt and chunks of wood. Burns dived across the tunnel floor, rolling. He fired a blast from his shotgun, racked it, kicking out an empty shell. He fired again, and the shotgun was empty. He tossed it aside, and pulled his .45, firing into the dark.

Burns pointed with his left hand to Ruggieri, who moved up along the tunnel wall and crouched near one of the heavy beams. He opened fire with his Uzi, spraying the tunnel and lighting it with the flickering strobe of the muzzle flashes.

Burns leaped to his feet and ran forward as Ruggieri stopped firing and rose to follow him. They hurried along the smoky tunnel, not seeing anything in front of them, but able to hear someone moving.

* * *

Far ahead of them, Gavril and Wynter ran up the ramp that led to the outside. Wynter climbed into the cab of the van and turned, looking over the backseat at Halloran. She leaned on it, resting her left arm, and pointed her pistol at Halloran, almost as if wishing he would try something. She was breathing hard, the sweat dripping from her face and staining the light-colored blouse she wore. Even with the breath rasping in her throat, she grinned at Halloran.

Gavril got in the other side, pulled a key from his pocket, and started the van. He backed up, turned it around so that it was facing out of the alley and sitting next to the exit from the tunnel. He was waiting for Jihar, who had disappeared inside again.

Jihar stopped near the door and jerked several strips of wood from the tunnel wall. There was a compartment hidden there, cut into the earth. He reached in and pulled the small, hand-held generator from its hiding place. With his other hand, he patted the bottom of the compartment, located the lead wires, and yanked them free. Quickly, he connected them to the terminals on the generator. He checked the wires to make sure they were seated properly and then grinned down the tunnel as he twisted the crank, once, twice, three times to make sure that he got a good electrical burst.

Burns was still running along the tunnel wall when the world seemed to blow up in front of him. He dived back, rolled once, and then watched as part of the tunnel ceiling dropped, the dirt cascading down with it, obscuring everything. Burns got to his feet, took a step forward, and realized that the tunnel was effectively blocked. The explosion had not been designed to kill any pursuers but to stop the pursuit. Burns didn't waste time. He turned and ran back the way he had come, knowing that it was fruitless. By the time he could get back up to street level, the terrorists he had been chasing would be long gone— out of the area and scattered throughout the city, or heading to a secret camp and Burns had no idea where it might be.

As he reached James and Ruggieri, he gestured to them and continued running, knowing that it was hopeless, that he had lost his one piece of intelligence of any real value. He would have to start over, trying to learn where the terrorists might go to hide. He would hear from them, he was sure.

CHAPTER EIGHT

While Burns, James, and Ruggieri were running through the tunnel in the basement of the terrorists' tenement, Ambassador Virgil Morgan was returning to the embassy. The long, black limousine with its blue pennant attached to the front fender stopped briefly while a Jemali guard opened the wrought-iron gate, and then entered the grounds. The limousine turned to the left and stopped as close to the front entrance as it could get. The driver leaped out and opened the rear door for the ambassador. Morgan got out, glanced up at the roof of the three-story building where an armed Marine guard roamed, then looked back at the main gate where a Jemali guard stood. He was worried about all the things that had happened recently. Worried about the kidnapping of the two Marines, the killing of one of them, the hijacking of the arms truck—all the recent trouble.

He reached back into the limousine and got his black briefcase. Straightening, he saw two secretaries crossing the courtyard and returned their waves. Both were young women at their first foreign posting and the ambassador worried about their safety. He wondered if he should order them, as well as most of the rest of the staff, out of the country. At the main door, he waited while the Marine guard, Corporal Josephson, reached under the desk to punch the button that would unlock the door. When he heard the buzz, he grabbed the door, let the secretaries enter, and then followed. He went straight to the elevator and took it up to his office.

As the ambassador disappeared, Josephson turned his attention to the screen of the TV monitor near him. He was looking at the main gate when an ambulance approached. It stopped at the gate and the Jemali guard, rather than opening up, walked through the pedestrian entrance to the side of the vehicle. He looked through the windshield at the driver, and then moved to the window on the driver's side of the cab. He leaned close, said something, shook his head, and returned to the gatehouse.

He called Josephson on the field phone in his hut and told him what the driver had said. "Medical supplies?" Josephson said. "Didn't hear a thing about medical supplies. Hold on and I'll check upstairs."

Josephson grabbed another phone, pushed a button, and was surprised when the ambassador himself answered. He told Morgan what he had learned from the Jemali guard at the main gate.

"Absolutely not," the ambassador told him. "Somebody's really flubbed this time."

Josephson thanked the ambassador and hung up. He picked up the other phone and told the Jemali guard, "They say no, it's a mistake."

The Jemali nodded and hung up. He walked back out the gate and looked up at the driver, repeating the message. The man shrugged as if he didn't have a care in the world. Smiling at the Jemali, he removed his cap to wipe the sweat from his forehead and said something about the heat and bureaucratic foul-ups.

He glanced to his right while talking to the guard, and picked up the pistol sitting there. Then, using his cap to hide the gun from the TV cameras mounted near the gate, he aimed his pistol at the Jemali.

To the Jemali guard, the ambulance driver hissed, "Open the gate."

In the embassy building, Josephson watched the exchange on his TV monitor. He didn't understand why the guard was taking so long, and wished that he would just send the ambulance away. Josephson didn't like things out of the ordinary because they usually blew up in someone's face. He saw the Jemali turn away and then was surprised as the Jemali opened the main gate.

The ambulance driver didn't hesitate. He accelerated through the gate, picking up speed as he raced across the compound. Josephson reached out, punched the button hidden under his desk, and leaped for the front door, drawing his weapon. He stepped out, held the .45 in both hands and aimed at the driver's side of the ambulance. He squeezed off two rounds and then had to dive to the side.

The ambulance didn't slow and didn't waver. It climbed the steps up to the main entrance and crashed into the glass and steel of the door. Josephson was clipped by the ambulance as he tried to get clear. The impact spun him around and he landed hard, banging his head, stunning himself.

The sound of the crash burst through the embassy. The people, the clerks, the secretaries, the attachés, and the guards all heard it and poured into the hallways, asking one another what had happened. Two of the Marines, weapons drawn, headed for the open elevator. The ambassador stuck his head into the hall, watched the people milling about, shouting at one another, and then ducked back into his office where he could find out what was going on. He grabbed the phone, trying to raise the Marine at the front desk.

In the ambulance, the man, his face bloodied by flying glass from the shattered windshield, shook himself and remembered the words Jihar had spoken to him. That he was a valued member of the rebel organization. He remembered the humiliation in the jail cell, the other men who thought that he was crazy, deluded, or maybe both. Now he would show them all. He would gain his place in heaven by his act of self-sacrifice, his death in a holy war.

Hamed reached for the ring that was where the cigarette lighter should have been. He hooked his finger through it, grinned upward at the sky, thinking about heaven, and jerked the ring.

The blast broke windows for a fifty-block radius around the embassy. The force of the explosion shook the building, blew out a gigantic chunk of the front wall, and blasted a hole in the second and third floor, creating a crater nearly thirty feet across. Part of the walls and structural support collapsed, the stone, furniture, and people cascading down in a huge cloud of dust, dirt, and debris. The flash started fires throughout the embassy, burning the carpets, the wooden furniture, the wall coverings, the paint. Flames shot through the hole in the second floor and up into the third. Smoke filled the building in seconds.

There was a moment of silence in the embassy as everything in every corner of the building came to stop, and then a single, piercing scream. A scream that came from the bowels of the building. It was as if that scream triggered an eruption. People started running everywhere, shouting at one another. They began to drag the bodies of the injured from where they fell, tried to revive the unconscious and stop the bleeding of the wounded. There were demands for first-aid kits, for the embassy doctor, and then for ambulances to transport the badly injured to local hospitals. In those first few minutes, no one knew what had happened, who had died, who was on the embassy grounds and who wasn't, or what they should do during the next few minutes. Everyone was waiting for someone else to take charge and tell them what to do. Only a few ran screaming from the building. Those who weren't injured tried to help those who were.

Halfway across the city, Burns, Ruggieri, and James were in their jeep, returning from the morning raid. They heard the echo of the explosion as it rocked the city, reverberating back and forth, and saw the billowing cloud of black smoke and brown dust as it boiled above the buildings.

Burns slowed down so that he could study the scene in front of him, suddenly sure of what it meant. A terrorist attack on the embassy itself. No longer a covert war of political intrigues and one or two deluded people trying to take out one or two others. No longer a war of words between the terrorists and the politicians, but a real war of bombs and guns directed at the Americans.

He glanced at Ruggieri, who sat beside him in the jeep. Ruggieri's face was a mask, a shocked mask drained of blood, staring at the evidence of the attack as it climbed higher into the morning sky.

Behind him James muttered something unintelligible. Burns looked over his shoulder and saw James watching the ground, as if he couldn't believe what he had seen and by not watching it, he could make it go away. It was the second time in two days he had seen the bury-your-head-in-the-sand syndrome.

Burns shifted into a lower gear and hit the accelerator, ignoring the traffic around him. He dodged around trucks, pushcarts loaded with food and fruits, and people who scampered out of his way when they saw him coming. He spun the wheel, avoiding a truck stalled in the center of the cobblestone street, turned a corner and looked into the distance where he could see the burning front of the embassy, the wide crater that still smoked, and a couple of smaller shapes that had to be bodies of people killed in the blast. Already a crowd was gathering to watch as sirens wailed in the distance, signaling the first of the help to arrive.

Elli Bauman was shaken awake by the explosion. At first she didn't know what had happened. She leaped from bed, went to the window of her hotel room, and looked out on the street. She could see dozens of people below her running in every direction, shouting at each other, and pointing in all directions as they tried to learn what had just blown up.

She looked across the tops of the buildings and saw the black cloud rising above the American Embassy. She watched it gain altitude for a moment and then heard the emergency sirens begin: distant, lonesome wailings from a single vehicle were joined by another and another, as if the explosion had awakened them too.

There was a knock at her door and she turned to look at it as if that would tell her who was there. She glanced at her bed, picked up her robe, and put it on since she was wearing as little as possible because of the heat of the desert air and the lack of air conditioning in the hotel. As she fastened it, the knock came again and she moved to the door. She took off the chain, letting it drop, turned the dead bolt, and opened it.

For just an instant she stood there stunned, staring into the faces of the three people there. Then she moved back, out of the way and let Maude Wynter and her two rebel friends into the room. Once they were inside, she closed the door and locked it before turning around to confront them. Each of them held a small-caliber pistol.

The front of the embassy had caved in. Part of the facade had collapsed, revealing all of the floors of the three-story building. Support beams could be seen, twisted out of shape and sticking up at crazy angles. There was furniture visible in the rubble, some of it damaged so heavily that it was barely recognizable and some of it looking practically new. There were heating pipes and cooling ducts exposed to the air and bent and broken water pipes, some of them spraying streams of water into the air, giving small portions of the wreckage an almost festive atmosphere.

People scrambled over the wreckage like ants near an overturned picnic basket. Jemali soldiers, distinctive in their khaki uniforms and kaffiyeh, were digging through the ruins, and had formed a human chain to lift and toss chunks of cement, blocks, and beams to the ground, out of the way. Others used shovels and crowbars, or just their bare hands, to dig and pry through the debris, none of them talking but all of them digging rapidly.

Red Cross personnel wearing white shirts and white pants were helping the soldiers dig, or were treating the wounded who were still on the embassy ground, giving them medication, wrapping them with bandages, and comforting them. They had moved the dead to a corner of the parking lot and covered the bodies with whatever was handy. Towels, blankets, and sheets that were now blood-soaked covered the dead, keeping the sun, the vultures, the insects, and the prying eyes of the news media off them. Other Red Cross volunteers were handing out coffee and sandwiches to the workers, coordinating the rescue effort, requesting more aid, more equipment, more people. More everything.

The Marines were there, too. Burns shoved against a massive crossbeam, the cords standing out on his neck, the muscles in his arms flexing and rippling as he pushed. James and Ruggieri were at the ends of the beam, lifting, straining, pushing. Together the three of them shifted the beam to the left out of the way. Just a couple of feet below, they spotted a hand protruding from the wreckage. It was wedged between two gigantic pieces of flooring that were held apart by cinder blocks, floor joists, and beams.

For an instant they stopped and stared. Ruggieri called out, but there was no response. He listened, concentrating as he waved his arm for silence. The hand looked pale, drained of blood. Ruggieri grabbed one of the crowbars, jammed it into the debris and lifted while James reached under and tried to roll the wreckage clear. Burns leaped over to assist and the combination of Ruggieri on the crowbar with Burns and James lifting let them push the flooring to the side.

Burns reached down as the rest of the arm became visible, to help drag the body out, but his hand stopped in midair. He could see the hand, wrist, elbow, and shoulder: that was it. There was no body, just the bloodied shoulder joint where there should have been more. There was a smear of blood on the debris, but he couldn't tell if the stain was from the shoulder or from the man crawling away. Burns looked up at Ruggieri, the effort of holding back the debris etched on his face, and shook his head. Ruggieri understood immediately and let the rubble fall back with a loud bang. Smoke boiled out of the tiny opening and the three of them moved down to the ground, looking for a place where their help was needed immediately.

Ambassador Morgan was wandering the grounds, dazed, his eyes unseeing. He staggered like a man drunk, weaving from the hastily covered bodies to the Red Cross rescue vehicles parked on the lawn and toward the people who were digging. He staggered in wide circles without a destination, as if he were trying to see everything.

Burns saw him, saw a trickle of blood from his head wound as he stared at the disaster, and moved to him.

"Where's the colonel?" asked the ambassador, his words slightly slurred. He didn't look at Burns but kept talking to him. "He's not here. Have you seen the colonel? He's under here, isn't he? Tell me the truth. He's buried under all this."

"No, Mr. Ambassador, the colonel isn't here," said Burns gently, quietly. "He may not even be dead."

"That's right, they took him." The ambassador faced Burns and asked, "Who are all these people who do this? Savages. We've got to get our people out. We've been ordered to evacuate all American personnel from Jemal."

Burns shook his head. "We don't have all our people back yet." He wanted to remind the ambassador that Colonel Halloran was missing, but knew that the ambassador was aware of that.

"We can't wait. We've got to get them out." The ambassador's voice rose with each word.

"You should see to that head wound, Mr. Ambassador," said Burns.

"Wound?" He looked puzzled and then touched his head. He looked at the blood staining his hand, wiped the blood on his suit coat, and said, "So much blood. Why?"

"Maybe because it's so cheap here." He took the ambassador's elbow, trying to steer him away from the rubble-choked front of the embassy. He spotted a Red Cross volunteer and raised a hand to get her attention.

"Help the ambassador," he said to her. "He needs some attention."

She nodded and reached out, putting her hand on the ambassador's shoulder, helping him toward one of the ambulances parked nearby.

As they moved across the lawn, stepping over some of the debris, Burns saw an Arab boy push through the pedestrian gate and run toward him. The boy was wearing a dirty, cotton shirt and ragged pants, with sandals on his feet.

When he was close, he asked, "Sergeant Burns?"

Burns nodded and said, "Yes?"

"An old peddler told me to tell you if you want to know who did this to come to the fruit warehouse in the marketplace." Having delivered his message, the boy turned and ran off without waiting for any kind of tip, back through the gate and into the street, disappearing rapidly into the crowd.

Burns turned and saw Ruggieri and James digging through the rubble, both working hard, working fast; throwing pieces of the debris aside, trying to work their way deeper, toward the interior of the building.

Burns walked closer to them and when he had their attention, said, "You two, listen up. We've been ordered to evacuate. I want you two to help get all the embassy personnel down to the airport, help with the medical, that sort of thing. Any questions?"

"What about the colonel, Gunny?" James asked, dusting the palms of his hands together. He was covered with dirt and grime, the sweat cutting streaks through it. With his forearm he touched his face, wiping the sweat from it.

"We're moving everybody out," Burns said flatly. He stared at them, daring them to say something about the order. It wasn't an order that Burns liked because it seemed that they were running out. That the terrorists had won. But it was an order that he could do nothing about.

"You gonna meet us there at the airport?" asked Ruggieri, wiping his forehead on the sleeve of his fatigues. His face was still smeared with the camo paint they had put on the night before. He was breathing hard from the exertion of digging through the piles of rubble in the desert heat. He leaned against the handle of the shovel for support.

"I'll be there," Burns said, nodding. "But I want your asses on that plane when I get there. Got it?"

He stared at them, waiting for their response. When both of them nodded, he climbed down from the rubble and walked slowly across the lawn. He detoured toward the jeep he had been driving that morning and got one of the shotguns out of the back of it. He passed the ambulance with its rear door open, where the ambassador was sitting with a young man dressed in bloodstained whites dabbing at the ambassador's head. Burns continued walking across the parking lot, where the bodies of the dead were lined up for identification and evacuation. He glanced at the tarps covering the bodies. From under one of them he could see a pair of small feet. There was a high-heel shoe on one foot and several toes missing from the other. He just kept going, not wanting to see any more, until he reached the shattered front gate.

There were large crowds still gathered outside the gate, staring at the ruined embassy building. There were several Marine guards at the gate, each armed with an M16 or shotgun, standing behind wooden barricades, their eyes on the people. They had been reinforced by Jemali soldiers and police. Burns pushed by them, nodded to them, and then melted into the crowd, not sure what he would find at the marketplace. He just knew that he had to go to learn if the fruit peddler knew anything of importance. The colonel was still missing and Burns had no intention of leaving Jemal without the colonel.

CHAPTER NINE

The walk to the marketplace took less than twenty minutes. Burns moved along the streets and alleys easily, the people around him either heading toward the damaged embassy or intent on not meeting his eyes. One or two looked at the shotgun he carried, but armed men on the streets, especially men in uniform, were not an uncommon sight.

He turned into the marketplace, where he could see hundreds of people: people bartering with one another, arguing over the price of goods, the price of food, offering trades, trying to get more money, or pay less. There were men with pushcarts, shoving them through the streets, shouting that they had the best fruit or nuts or meats. A man with several carpets demanded Burns's attention, but Burns walked by him without seeing him. Iron Monger Jim from Anoka announced to all in the vicinity that he had the finest blades available anywhere. An old woman held a long-handled pot with something steaming in it for Burns to see and smell, telling him that it was the best of whatever it was, a treat fit for Allah: she neglected to tell him what it was.

To one side was a new, brightly colored awning that sloped from a balcony on one of the buildings.

A man stood under it, shouting and pointing to a young woman who stood on a raised platform. She was fully clothed, with a dense veil over her face and her hair covered. The only thing that Burns could see were her big, dark eyes. He wasn't sure what the man was telling him.

Burns pushed by and turned another corner so that he stood in front of the produce warehouse, a large stone building that seemed to be deserted. There were a couple of empty pushcarts near the doors; empty boxes stained with the juice of the fruit that had been packed in them were scattered in the dirt; bits of broken fruit were everywhere. The windows were all closed, the doors all seemed barred, and the single wooden stairway led to a door that looked as if it had been nailed shut. There was no one anywhere to be seen, though he could hear the people of the marketplace around the corner.

Burns walked to the closest door, twisted the knob, and pushed. It swung open silently. The interior was dim and warm, but he could see a flickering light from deep inside. He entered cautiously. The building seemed to be as empty as the street outside it. There were more empty boxes and more litter on the floor, but there was no produce in the warehouse. No sounds came from the interior and it seemed the warehouse was as deserted as the street outside it. There were torches around the walls that caused the flickering light Burns had seen from the door. He stepped forward, studying the interior.

Around the walls there were dark places that seemed to be alcoves. Burns had no idea what they were for. The shadows danced on the floor and wall as the breeze from the open door blew through and fanned the flames of the torches.

From far behind him, Burns heard the quiet scrape of shoe leather on the floor. Burns glanced over his shoulder and then turned. The man behind him held an automatic weapon, a short stocky thing that was either an Uzi or an Ingram Model 10, though in the half-light of the warehouse, it was hard to tell which. He stared at it for a moment, deciding that it had to be an Uzi. It seemed to be slightly larger than an Ingram should have been.

Off to the right, there was movement and another man appeared from another of the darkened alcoves. Burns looked at him, and took a step back, deeper into the warehouse. A third man entered through the door, as if he had been following Burns through the marketplace. Holding his Remington shotgun in both hands, the barrel parallel with the floor, he looked from one man to the next.

From behind him came a voice that he recognized: the voice of the man who had brought the gold wings to the embassy, the voice of the man who had sketched the rebel headquarters, the voice of the man who had worked the streets, shouting that he had fresh fruit for sale—the voice of a man who seemed to be everywhere that there was some action involving the terrorists and the Americans.

"Would you like some fruit, Sergeant?" the voice asked him quietly.

Burns spun, his shotgun ready. A tall, well-built man with dark hair and a long, angular face stood there. He was younger than the old fruit peddler should have been, not more than thirty-five. He was now dressed in a khaki uniform with epaulets and short sleeves, having given up his robes and kaffiyeh. He had on desert boots and held an Uzi.

"Who the hell are you?" demanded Burns.

"I am Elias, a harmless fruit peddler, remember?" he said with a mock bow. "You can put down your weapon. If we wanted to kill you, you'd be dead now. We're the Mossad."

"Israeli Intelligence?" Burns glanced at the other men, who had moved back into the shadows.

"That's right," confirmed Elias.

"So," Burns said. "I'm impressed with your makeup job. Now what's on your mind?"

"Elli Bauman," Elias said. He noticed the look on Burns's face and added quickly, "She's my sister and one of us."

Burns took in the information, wondered about it, because she had seemed to be working against him at every move, seemed to be working for the terrorists. It was the perfect cover. It had fooled him completely and apparently worked as well on the terrorists. Finally he asked, "What's that got to do with me and my people?"

"The terrorists have taken her. We believe she is being held in the same place as your colonel, the place where the suicidal terrorist who blew up your embassy came from."

Burns nodded, slipped on the safety of his shotgun, and moved closer to Elias. "I suppose you have a plan."

Jihar's headquarters at the rebel camp was in a single-story building made of dust-colored stone. It was a long, flat building with a short wall around the roof, a couple of palm trees to the side, and a dozen rooms inside, a couple of them fitted with electric lights. On top, there were two rebel guards, each carrying a Soviet-made AK-47 with a thirty-round banana clip. They wore dark-colored uniforms and had their faces hidden by their headgear. They kept moving because they had been told they would be shot if they fell asleep, and they might be shot just for sitting down.

Below them a single guard, dressed the same way, stood outside the door to the building. He stood at a modified parade rest, his AK held in both hands across his chest. He didn't turn his head, but kept his eyes roaming the open, flat ground that led to a short stone wall. No one dared enter the area without permission. The guard, however, did not have a magazine in his weapon. He had one banana clip stuck in the right pocket of his pants.

Inside, Jihar sat behind his desk in his office. He held a pencil in one hand, which he tapped impatiently on the edge of his old, scarred desk. The top of it was empty. A couple of old, wooden chairs stood to one side, but no one sat in either of them. There was a bookcase near the chairs with nearly a hundred poorly printed and badly bound manuals and books in it. Behind him was a large rebel flag. It looked as if it had hung in the room for a long time.

Standing to one side, out of the way and leaning against the wall, were Karl Gavril and Maude Wynter. Neither said anything; they were there as observers. Wynter fanned herself slowly with a folded magazine. Her hair was damp with sweat and there were stains under her arms.

Elli sat in an uncomfortable wooden chair that was in the center of the room, isolated from everything else. She had dressed in a white cotton blouse, now wet under the arms and down the back, and a khaki skirt that came to her knees. There were scuffed brown boots on her feet.

For a moment she stared at Jihar, and then waved

a hand in frustration. "Is this an interrogation, Jihar? Is it? After the risks I have taken on behalf of your organization, how can you presume?" She stopped talking, a look of bewilderment on her face. "Why?"

Jihar tossed the pencil to the top of the desk, watching it roll and then disappear as it fell to the dirty, flagstone floor. "We presume nothing, Miss Bauman. But every one of us is subject to an investigation." He waved at Gavril and Wynter, a gesture that might have included everyone in the camp, and then added quickly, "When irregularities occur... betrayals... an investigation is necessary."

Bauman glanced at the two terrorists standing near the wall, and then looked back at Jihar. "I have never betrayed you," she said firmly. "Never."

"My dear Elli," Gavril said, stepping away from the wall, "that you are alive and with us, participating in the investigation, demonstrates our willingness to believe you." He turned toward Wynter and then back to Bauman. "Perhaps you have omitted something that you felt was unimportant. Perhaps you have forgotten—"

"I have forgotten nothing!" she snapped, staring at him. "I have omitted nothing."

"You met twice with Sergeant Burns, the American Marine," Jihar reminded her.

"And told him only what I was instructed. I gave him useless photographs," she countered. She wanted to wipe the perspiration from her face but was afraid the movement would be misinterpreted, might be seen as nervousness or fear on her part.

"Yet he acquires intelligence concerning the precise location of our hostage," Jihar said evenly. "Does he imagine this? Unlikely."

"I have told him nothing. Only what I was instructed to tell him."

Gavril pulled a chair away from the wall, dragged it closer to Bauman, and sat down. Smiling at her, he took her hand in both of his. "Elli, a disturbing recollection has recently begun to haunt me." He frowned at her. "You recall our departed colleague, Herr Kroger? How he died?"

"Yes," Elli said, nodding slightly, her voice edged with emotion as she remembered. "The Mossad. They are ruthless fanatics. But—"

"Of course it is merely coincidental that you interviewed him shortly before his assassination." He shrugged as if dismissing the idea himself, as if it were an idea without merit. "But when coincidence accumulates, one is liable to suspect a grand design."

Bauman jerked her hand away from him, outraged. She looked at Jihar, who was sitting quietly, listening. "What are you saying?" she demanded. "Do you think—" She felt tears burn her eyes suddenly and choked back a sob. "I was in love with Hans."

"And I believe you, Elli," Gavril said, standing. He put a hand on her shoulder as if to reassure her. "I merely point out the possible interpretations."

Bauman buried her face in her hands as her shoulders shook and she began to cry, almost hysterically. She bent over, her breath ragged and strained as the sobs racked her body, leaving her almost helpless.

Gavril looked at the others and shrugged. He didn't know whether or not to believe her and saw that the others were equally puzzled. All they had were a couple of half-baked notions that could be totally wrong, and a member of the working press was too valuable an ally to kill without being sure that she was a traitor to their cause. He watched her cry for a moment and then stepped behind her chair so that he could touch her shoulder to comfort her.

In the produce warehouse, Burns stood staring at several maps spread out on a couple of old crates. There were maps of the surrounding countryside, maps of the city, and maps of the interiors of buildings. The Mossad agents had gathered around and were studying the maps, too.

"Though Elli was blindfolded when she was taken to their camp," explained Elias, "we were able to put together their location by her pictures. It's a monastery high in the mountains."

Burns traced a road along the map with his fingers, following the route up into the mountains, and then asked, "What kind of resistance can we expect?"

Elias shrugged and then said, "Maybe forty well-trained fanatics."

Burns looked around, staring at each of the men in the room with him. "I count eight of us."

"For an Israeli that makes it about even."

"What about weapons?" Burns asked.

Elias nodded and two of the men folded the maps and moved them out of the way. One of the men pulled the blankets away and then the other used a crowbar to pry open the tops of the crates. Once they were open, he stood back, out of the way.

Burns moved closer so that he could look into the crates. He walked around them slowly, inspecting the weapons, but didn't touch any of them. Occasionally he leaned close to study something, check a serial number or a manufacturer's stamp, see what caliber a rifle or submachine gun was. He was surprised by the numbers and kinds of weapons: M16s, M79 grenade launchers, a box of hand grenades, a crate of LAW rockets, and a box of several short, stubby-looking weapons that Burns didn't recognize.

"Jesus! You got a whole arsenal here. A dragon, saw automatic, mortars."

Elias looked at the boxes proudly and smiled at Burns. "The terrorists weren't the only ones who picked the Jemalis' pockets," he said.

Finally Burns reached out and touched one of the rifles, felt the light coating of oil on it, saw it shine in the flickering light of the warehouse, and then looked up at Elias. "Yeah," he said. "I like the odds."

CHAPTER TEN

The rooftop guards had been changed at sunset. There were still two on the top of Jihar's headquarters building, another outside the front door and still another in the back, hidden behind a scraggly bush of dried leaves that rattled in the light breeze. Across the way, not more than twenty or thirty feet, was the hostage hut. A guard had been stationed on top of it and another put on the only doorway. There were other guards stationed around the compound, a couple on the front gate, two more opposite them, one on top of the mess hall, and one each at the four corners of the base. Each of the guards, with the exception of the man hiding in the bush, could be seen by the others.

Inside the hostage hut, two of the terrorists sat at a small table. Both were dressed in dirty khakis, an OD green pistol belt around their waists holding .45 automatics. Each was wearing a kaffiyeh that hid his face so that Halloran wouldn't recognize them if he somehow escaped. They doubted that he would. One of them held a die while the other looked on. They were playing backgammon, and the one man had just doubled, to the amusement of his partner.

On the floor near the back wall, where there were

no windows and the only exit was through the door that was blocked by the table and guards, was Halloran. He was still wearing his torn, stained, dirty uniform. There were bruises on his face and dried blood on his clothes. He was bound, hands behind his back and ankles roped to them. He was sleeping fitfully, dozing actually, jerking awake every few minutes and then drifting off again.

Almost everyone else, with the exception of the guards on duty, was asleep. In Jihar's headquarters building, Bauman was asleep on a metal cot with a paper-thin mattress. In her sleep, she cried out once, and then mumbled, "Hans. Hans Kroger." She kicked the light sheet from her, wrapping it around her ankles. She flipped to a side, mumbled again, and then rolled onto her back.

Suddenly, she was wide awake, sitting up, her breath rasping in her throat. She felt the sweat trickling down her face, down her sides, and beading between her breasts. She stared into the dark, the images of her dreams swirling in front of her as she tried to remember where she was and what she was doing. In the dark around her, she heard a metallic click, and everything rushed back. She turned slowly, staring.

Maude Wynter was watching her from her own cot a few feet away, supported on one elbow, her Walther in her hand, aimed at Bauman. Bauman could just make Wynter out, a dark shape in low-cut white, a sheet at her waist, her light hair hanging in her face. She brushed it back with that hand that held her weapon, and then pointed it back at Bauman, as if daring her to try something.

On the other side of Wynter, Gavril slept on,

snoring quietly. He was little more than a dark lump on his cot, almost invisible in the night, undisturbed by the noise that Bauman had been making.

For several seconds, Bauman stared at Wynter, and then lay back, rolled to her side, and closed her eyes. She deepened her breathing, as if she had fallen back to sleep, then opened her eyes, watching the blank wall. She waited patiently, listening for sounds from Wynter.

Finally, she heard the metal of Wynter's cot groan as the woman shifted into a more comfortable position and carefully lowered the hammer of her weapon. There was a momentary stirring, as Wynter settled herself into her cot.

Several hours later, at the produce warehouse in the marketplace, Burns picked up his shotgun and headed for the door. He stopped for a moment and glanced at the sky. He could see the fingers of pink and gray as the dawn chased back the night. The stars were slowly fading. There was a breeze from the ocean that smelled of salt and fish.

Burns stopped moving and saw Ruggieri sitting on a wooden crate, dressed in sweatstained tiger-striped fatigues with a pistol belt and harness. His rifle was sitting butt first on the ground, the barrel against his leg. He was eating a Snickers bar. Standing next to him, a rifle leaning against him, was James. He too wore fatigues and a combat pack. He was watching a couple of peddlers moving into position for the new day.

Burns moved to the Marines and asked, "Okay, how'd you two find me?"

Ruggieri pulled back the brown wrapper of his

candy bar, took a big bite, and as he chewed said, "Kids will tell you anything for some pogey, Gunny." He smiled and held up the candy bar.

"I thought I told you two to be on that plane," Burns said quietly.

"We got all embassy people aboard. That cargo plane left last night." Ruggieri smiled and added, "Early last night. Hours ago."

Burns looked from one man to the other but didn't speak to either of them. Finally Ruggieri broke the silence, saying, "We ain't going without you and the colonel, Gunny."

"You know we're all probably going to get court-martialed for this."

"Semper fi, Gunny," said Ruggieri. He finished his candy bar, looked for a place to throw away the wrapper, and then wadded it into a small ball, tossing it to the already littered ground, shrugging.

"Okay," Burns said. "Just watch your asses."

James picked up his rifle, Ruggieri shouldered his, and they began moving toward the jeep. Burns watched them for a moment, wondering if he shouldn't order them to the airfield to wait for him, but suddenly understood what they were thinking about. It was the same thing he thought about. Nobody, not the ambassador, the embassy staff, the State Department, or the U.S. Government was going to take care of them. They had to do it themselves. They were all alone on this one. Burns felt he had to go find the colonel. Ruggieri and James felt they had to stick by their gunnery sergeant, and if the colonel was rescued in the process, so much the better. It was a loyalty among the Marines that many of the outsiders couldn't or wouldn't understand.

He got into the jeep, started the engine, and turned

around so that he could head to the staging area.
There Elias had arranged for transport that would get
them to the rebel's camp so they could begin the
assault.

Shortly before dusk, a nondescript Land Rover
left the capital city, traveling along the narrow
streets, the paved highways, and dirt roads, speeding
up toward the rebel's mountain camp. In the backseat, Amin, the Jemali Minister of Finance, sat
watching the desert slide by. Amin looked out the
front as the driver, Mustafa, downshifted and
touched the brake, slowing them.

Ahead of them, a truck had pulled off the road. It
was sitting there, the hood up, a cloud of steam rising from it. A man was bent over the fender, his
head hidden in the engine compartment.

As they approached, the man apparently heard
them and straightened. He waved at them, a look of
frustration on his grease-smeared face, a wrench held
in one hand. When they went by, Mustafa shot a
glance at the rearview mirror, to watch the action of
the stranded man, who had just watched them as if
he had expected them to stop to help. Mustafa didn't
recognize the old fruit peddler.

They left the desert then, the road disintegrating
into an ill-defined path, and began a slight climb that
gradually became steeper as they drove higher. The
road on one side dropped away, revealing the
boulder-strewn landscape dotted with dried vegeta-
tion, reaching for the sandy valley floor below. Rising on the other side was a stone cliff that sprouted a
few shriveled bushes. In the fading light of the sun,
it was increasingly hard to see the landscape. The

shadows crept down the side of the mountain to enshroud the road with darkness.

They reached a wide, gentle curve where the road vanished around the side of the mountain. As they drove around it, they saw two terrorist guards standing in the road. Both were armed with AK-47s with banana clips, wearing khaki uniforms with kaffiyehs that wrapped around their heads and draped around their faces to hide them.

One of them recognized the Land Rover. He touched the other on the shoulder and both men moved back, stepping out of the way so that the car could pass. High above them, on an outcropping of rock was another lone guard. His position let him see the whole valley and road. With a grenade launcher and a high-powered rifle, he could stop a battalion long enough for the terrorists in the camp to escape. That was, if he saw them coming and knew what they were.

Lying on a ridge line below them, the man who had been working on his stranded truck when Amin drove past in his Land Rover lowered his binoculars. He had seen the Land Rover pass through the road-block, seen the guard on the cliff. And in the last of the sunlight he could see a man climbing the sheer rock face below the guard.

Gunnery Sergeant Jack Burns was slowly climbing higher on the cliff. Elias couldn't understand how he was doing it. From his vantage point, there seemed to be no hand- or footholds, just the unblemished face of stone. There were a few large protrusions, but they only concealed Burns's activity from the top and provided no help in the climb. In fact, during all the time that Elias had been watching, the guard on top of the cliff had yet to walk to the side to look over. Apparently he didn't believe that anyone could climb the sheer face of the cliff either.

"Amazing," Elias said. "Simply amazing."

He raised the binoculars to his eyes again and watched as Burns grabbed on to something and lifted himself up another three feet. He saw Burns's left foot seem to break free, kick out, and then find a hold on the rock. Burns looked back over his shoulder, and then up toward his destination far above him.

Elias lowered the binoculars, turned and then looked through them at the valley floor, hidden from the guard on the rock by the ridge where he was. On the valley floor, almost entirely wrapped in the shadows, he could see a Huey helicopter crouching, its rotors spinning slowly. James and Ruggieri, unrecognizable because of the distance, were stretching rope from the open cargo compartment. Once they had it pulled taut, at perpendicular angles to the helicopter, they began picking it up slowly, coiling it carefully because they would be using it to rappel into the rebel camp once the assault started.

Elias crawled back away from the crest of the ridge, then got to his feet so that he could return to the road. There he found his truck waiting, the hood down, the steam from the radiator long cleared away, and the hose that he had loosened to create the steam clamped back. He looked through the passenger side window and saw the driver was already in place, waiting to start the engine. Elias opened his door, climbed in, and nodded at the man.

"It's time to go. Sergeant Burns is almost there. We must take out the road guards now."

The driver didn't say a word. He grinned and started the engine, slipping the truck into gear.

* * *

At the terrorist camp, Jihar was in his office, sitting at his desk and looking at Gavril, tapping the end of his pencil on the edge of his desk. Gavril was sitting in one of the metal folding chairs, his eyes on Jihar, his legs crossed so that his foot danced with impatience, but not saying much. He was waiting for the arrival of the Minister of Finance.

Outside, they heard the Land Rover pull up and the engine die. The night was quiet, except for the voices of the rebels as they moved about the camp, the sounds of the insects that were beginning their nocturnal activities, and the cries of animals on the far side of the base. They heard the doors of the car slam and a burst of voices. A moment later Amin entered the office, Mustafa a pace behind him.

Amin saw Gavril and smiled at him, bowing slightly. "You have done well, Gavril. The Americans are evacuating—*have* evacuated."

"Surely not without their beloved colonel," Jihar asked sarcastically.

Amin looked at the big man and shook his head. "They will not negotiate for his release."

Jihar rose to his feet, his eyes blazing. He slammed a massive hand to the desk top, as if to get attention, and then said, "Just as well, then. He must die for Hamed." There was a hard edge to his voice.

"Not so fast, Jihar," said Gavril. "As long as we have the colonel, we must keep him as a symbol."

"Gavril is right," Amin said, nodding. He moved to a vacant chair and sat down. He studied the dirty room with distaste before he turned his attention on Jihar and added, "It not only embarrasses Nahir that his allies can do nothing. It makes him weaker and shows our people he has no power."

Jihar walked past the two men seated in front of him and went to the window. Outside, in the last of the sunlight, he could see many of his men as they moved across the compound toward the mess hall, some of them smoking, their cigarettes glowing. Most wore khaki uniforms, but some were dressed in civilian clothes. A few carried their weapons with them but most of them had left their guns in the quarters.

To his right he could see the hostage hut. The guard was still on the roof, but he had moved to the edge so that he too could see the men moving about below him. He could also see the man posted at the front of the hut, and the dim glow from the windows. He didn't like having so much light because the enemy could spot it, but then, a lack of light might have been worse, might have made the authorities wonder why no one lived in the abandoned monastery.

"Take heart, Jihar," Gavril said coolly. "When Nahir falls, you can give these Marines their colonel."

Jihar turned away from the window and looked at Gavril. Amin looked from one to the other and waited for them to hammer out their differences concerning the Marine colonel.

"In little pieces, of course," he said, smiling.

CHAPTER ELEVEN

Elias sat in the front of the truck, a foot up on the dashboard as they worked their way up the mountain road, the engine grumbling under the strain. The driver downshifted and put his foot to the floor. The engine roared and the truck vibrated, but it didn't seem to pick up any speed as they climbed the hill toward the rebel camp.

They reached the long curve that would take them around the side of the mountain and up to the roadblock with the two terrorist guards. Elias let his foot drop to the floor and reached down to where he had a pistol hidden. He fingered it to make sure that it hadn't slipped away. When he felt the cold hardness of the weapon he smiled to himself. It wouldn't be long.

They stopped and the driver turned, pulling the wheel around, fighting it with both hands. He stopped, jammed it into reverse, then backed around the curve.

Elias looked into the rearview mirror on his side of the truck and saw the two terrorist guards leave their posts on the side of the road. They looked at one another and the rear of the truck and then began walking toward it slowly, warily, unsure of what they were seeing. Elias grinned at the mirror.

The guards halted and one of them shouted, but the driver ignored him, his foot on the gas, the truck backing up the road. The guard shouted again, and then moved his hand along the weapon, taking off the safety. He demanded that the truck stop, ordered it to stop at the top of his voice, or he would shoot.

The driver let his foot off the gas, shifted into neutral, and let the engine die. Once or twice he revved it. In the rearview mirror, he could see the two guards standing in the middle of the road, staring at the truck. He turned and grinned at Elias.

Elias shifted around in his seat so that he could look into the back of the truck. He shot a glance at the rearview mirror and heard the back doors of the truck open slowly. From the rear, there was a *pop,* like gasoline in a can suddenly igniting, and then a quiet *whoosh.* The back of the truck lit up as two jets of flame flashed out, funneling toward the guards, engulfing them.

Both men screamed in surprise and sudden pain. One of them took off running, waving his arms. He threw his rifle to the ground where the wooden stock continued to burn. He ran at the stone wall of the canyon, hit it, and bounced off, falling to his side. He began to roll then, leaving a trail of flaming jellied gasoline behind him. He reached out with a blackened hand, the fingers burned away. He grasped one of the tar-covered wooden supports for the metal railing, setting it on fire. He kept screaming.

The other man stood rooted to his spot for a moment, staring at the flaming death that poured from the back of the truck until his eyeballs melted.

Blinded, he staggered to the right, dropping his rifle as his hands burned away. The rounds in the bandoliers across his chest began to cook off. The tiny explosions would have burned him badly if he hadn't already been on fire. The bullets didn't have much force behind them as they punched into his feet and legs and the roadway near him. The tracers, glowing emerald green, landed near his feet as he staggered away, finally collapsing to the roadway.

The rear doors of the truck closed and the driver shifted into gear and began his ascent again. They passed the bodies, and Elias watched them recede, just two small piles of burning rags by the side of the road. Neither looked like a human being anymore.

Across the valley, on the other side of the mountain, Burns was struggling up the sheer cliff face, his arms outstretched as if he were embracing the rock. Just above him, twenty feet over his head, was a ridge, an outcropping of rock that was his goal. He glanced up at it, breathed out through his mouth, and wished that he could wipe the sweat from his forehead and face. He wished that he could sit down for a moment and take a drink of warm water from his canteen. He blinked his eyes rapidly, trying to keep the perspiration out of them, and felt it trickling down his face and back.

He slipped his feet along the crack in the rock, a tiny ledge that was just wide enough for the edges of his boots. He shifted to the left, slid his feet along, and reached out, grabbing at a protrusion from the cliff. His fingers caught a small hole in the stone and used it to pull himself along. He passed that, creeping along, the leather of his boots scraping at the rock. His face was pressed against the cliff so that he could see where he was going, but looked neither up nor down.

Slowly he worked his way along the ledge, getting closer to a crack that would allow him to finish the climb. He kept his eyes locked on that, an immediate goal that kept his mind off the rest of the climb. He didn't want to think about the next twenty feet or the guard that patrolled the top of the cliff. He only wanted to concentrate on the crack because it was close, because he could get to it quickly.

He shifted his weight again so that it was on his left foot. He heard a muffled *pop* and felt something slip. He heard a couple of rocks break loose, falling down, bouncing against the cliff, against outcroppings and boulders and the tiny, dried bushes until they had hit bottom several hundred feet below. He froze, felt his breath catch in his throat, forgetting to breathe for a moment. He leaned forward as far as he could, nearly pressing himself into the cliff, his face against the sun-hot rock. When nothing more happened, he began to move again, slowly sliding his feet along the tiny, fragile ledge.

Just at that moment, the ledge gave way. Burns began to topple, losing his balance in the sudden shift of the ledge. His left hand shot out, grabbing at air for an instant, and then he grabbed a dry, scraggly bush growing from the rock face. He caught it near the top and jerked himself upright. He held on to it tightly for a second and then let go, snagging it again, nearer to the thick, rough base. Now he looked down, felt a couple of rocks break free and tumble away. He watched them bouncing; each time they hit, they bounded out farther, taking pebbles and small stones with them. He lost sight of them in the shadows of the lower valley.

Burns felt the bush tremble and begin to pull free. He looked at it, saw the roots appear as they slipped out of the dirt in the crack. With his right hand, he reached into the cleft, trying to find something to hang on to, but the sides were too smooth and he could discover nothing to grab. He shoved his hand in deeper, feeling the rough rock. He pushed fingers through a narrow opening and felt it widen. Just as the bush pulled free, the roots letting go with an audible *pop* and the dirt cascading down, he balled his hand into a fist and wedged it deeply into the cleft.

He let go of the bush and it fluttered down, the dried leaves rattling in the air. Burns was practically hanging from the cliff by his right hand. He lifted his left foot, dragging it along the rock. He found a protrusion and tried to use it to take some of his weight, but it broke away. His foot slid down the rock again. He slowly raised his left foot, found another narrow ledge two or three inches wide, and set the edge of his foot against it. He levered himself up, felt the pressure released from his right hand. With his left, he reached above his head, found a crack that was big enough for a handhold, and grabbed it. When he felt himself stabilized, he pulled his right hand from the hole. He could feel an ache in it and felt scrapes on it from the rough rock.

He reached upward, over his head, his fingers dancing along the surface of the rock until he found a knotty protrusion. He grabbed it, lifted his right foot, and discovered a hole that he could get his toes into. He pushed, lifted himself up and began the climb again, slowly working his way higher. He found a rhythm and used it to climb. He was just under the top, protected from view by the outcropping that made it impossible for the guard to see him now that he had climbed so close to the plateau.

On the cliff top, a terrorist guard stood watch. He was wearing a khaki uniform, a pistol belt with a knife and a canteen, and had an AK-47 on a sling over his shoulder. He walked from one end of the plateau to the other, not really expecting to see anything in the valley because the floor was so far below that no one would be foolish enough to try to climb up the cliff. Periodically, he looked down anyway, just in case, but there was never anything to see, and now, with the sun fading, the light and shadows dancing across the cliff face, shifting and sliding, giving the rock a life that it did not have during the day or in the night, it would be impossible. Below him, he saw nothing.

He turned and headed toward the other end of the plateau only a couple of feet away. He could see into the camp and something down there caught his attention. He could see movement far below him, small figures, some of them recognizable and some of them wrapped in the anonymity of distance. He fingered a cigarette from a pack in his top pocket and lit it, tossing the match to the ground.

He knew that one of them below him was Elli Bauman, the dark-haired woman who had come into the camp a few days earlier. He wasn't sure if she was under guard for her protection or if it was for the protection of the camp. He watched her walk from the hostage hut to the mess hall, an armed guard at her side. They stopped once as the rebel pointed to something on the ground, but then continued until they were lost to sight.

He took a final drag on his cigarette, the glowing

tip drawing near his fingers so that he could feel the heat from it. He threw the cigarette to the ground and crushed it under his boot, grinding it into the dust to make it disappear completely. He turned then and looked toward the other end of this tiny plateau.

Burns had worked his way to the top of the cliff and was trying to lift himself up and over. He had his head and shoulders above the ground and had slid his knee up onto the top of the cliff.

The guard leaped forward and tried to kick Burns in the head. Burns saw the kick coming and ducked, dropping from sight as the sentry tried to nail him. The man's foot went high in the air and the momentum of the missed kick flipped him neatly skyward. The man fought to regain his balance, but couldn't do so. He hurtled outward, away from the cliff and into space. He grunted first and then realized what had happened. He screamed, a sound that bubbled in his throat and then rose in pitch until it sounded like the wail of a banshee.

Burns watched the man fly into space and then turned so that he could see the man flailing at the air, his arms windmilling and his legs kicking. His scream was cut off abruptly as he hit the side of the cliff, bounced, and continued his plunge to the valley far below.

Burns then moved again, his right foot pressed against a crack in the rock. He forced himself higher until he could plant his hands on the top of the cliff. He lifted, grunted, and rolled out onto the plateau. Slowly he got to his feet, brushed the dirt from the front of his uniform, and moved forward slightly so that he could see down into the rebel camp. He could see Elli Bauman leaving the mess hall, carrying a tray of food, one of the rebels with her. The man turned and looked up at Burns and then continued across the compound toward a small hut there, Bauman right beside him.

At the hostage hut, Bauman waited while the rebel opened the door. As she entered, she could see Halloran still bound to his chair, watching her, his eyes locked on hers. Maude Wynter stood at the small window, looking out into the compound, surveying everything out there as if she thought something was wrong and she was looking for it.

Bauman carried the tray to the tiny, rough table set to one side and put it down. She took a bowl from the tray, carried it to Halloran, sat down next to him to begin to feed him.

Wynter left her vantage point and sat at the table. She turned her plate around until the meat was directly in front of her and picked up a knife to cut it. She took a bite, put the knife down, and looked at the food as if it made her sick. She poked at it, studied it, and then put down her fork, as if resting between bites.

She watched Bauman feeding Halloran for a moment and then said, "Last night. You were talking in your sleep."

Bauman dipped a spoon into the bowl she held in her left hand and gave the food to Halloran. As he chewed, she glanced over her shoulder and said, "A nightmare." She set the bowl on the floor and moved to the table so that she could pour steaming tea into two big mugs. "I dreamed of Hans," she added. "Of his death."

Wynter picked up her fork, took another bite of the food, and chewed it slowly. Her eyes were on her plate for a moment and then she turned so that she could study Bauman. "You said a name. A name and other things," she said, watching for a reaction. "I didn't know that you spoke Hebrew."

Halloran noticed something pass between the two women. He wasn't sure what it was, but he watched them intently. He waited patiently, wondering just what was going on and wondering if he could use it to escape.

Bauman sipped her tea and found that it was too hot. She blew on it, her eyes on Wynter over the top of her cup. For a moment she said nothing and then: "I am fluent in several languages. I find it indispensable to my work."

"Yes. For your work." She stared at Bauman, the hostility on her face and in her eyes unmistakable. "I'm sure it's for your work."

Burns crouched near the side of the building, hidden in the shadows, and watched three rebels leave the mess hall, talking to one another, walking slowly toward the center of the compound. One of them glanced at the plateau, saw that no one was there and stopped walking. The other halted next to him as he pointed upward. For a second they just stared and then one of them turned and shouted at the guard who stood near the door of the hostage hut.

That man turned to look at the three and then spun so that he was facing the plateau, but could see no guard there either. He shrugged and then started off at a trot to investigate. The three rebels changed direction, too, running toward the hostage hut.

The lone man ran around the corner of a hut, slowed, as if wondering what to do, and then started to jog forward. As he passed Burns, concealed in the shadows of the hut and near a large bush that grew there, the Marine took a single step forward and swung both hands back over his own head, a thin nylon rope with wooden handles clenched in his fists. Burns snapped his arms down, throwing the garrote over the rebel's head and pulling it back and down. As the rope tightened around the man's throat and his hands came up to claw at it, Burns drove a knee into the terrorist's spine and pulled him back against him, driving his knee into the man. Then, bringing his elbows together, Burns spun left, crossing the rope over itself, as he bent sharply forward at the waist, straightening his legs and lifting the rebel's feet off the ground. Burns completed his movement by bringing the man over on his head in a throw designed to break the man's neck. He finished the attack by slamming a knee into the rebel's collarbone, breaking it, and pulling the garrote tight.

The rebel didn't understand what was happening to him. He felt the rope biting into his neck, felt the air to his lungs cut off and the flow of blood to his brain stopped. A curtain of black descended over him as he ripped at the rope with his own fingers, gouging himself and creating ribbons of blood. He kicked his feet, trying to hit his attacker as he lost consciousness. He never saw his killer and didn't feel any pain as Burns broke his collarbone.

When it was obvious that the man was dead, Burns loosened the garrote, wrapped it together, and slid it into a pocket. He took the dead man's rifle, extra ammunition, grenades, and knife. He pulled the body to the side, hiding it as best he could in the shadows of the hut behind the large bush that grew close to the wall.

Before he moved, he searched the ground directly in front of him. The three rebels had scattered and were out of sight. The area around him was vacant. Burns, keeping to the shadows, moved along the wall of the hut, his back to it, his eyes roving and his ears perked. He dodged from one hut to the next, running across the open ground in a half crouch, zigzagging in the shadows and the little cover available. He hit the wall of another hut, stopped, his back to it, and surveyed the ground around him. This hut seemed more substantial. The walls were stone, and still sun-warm. He remained there, listening before moving farther, but heard nothing. Finally, he began to jog along the wall, staying just far enough away so that he made no sound. He came to a corner and halted. There were no noises from the other side and he stepped around it.

Standing directly in front of him was one of the rebels. The man stood rooted to the ground, his eyes wide and unbelieving, his mouth open. He fumbled at the bolt of his weapon as if his fingers knew they were supposed to do something but were unsure what. Burns reacted immediately; he aimed a kick at the man's crotch and swung the butt of the rifle upward at his chest as the man began to double over. As the man collapsed to the dirt, Burns snapped the rifle down sharply, splintering the rebel's skull with a sickening crunch of bone. The man grunted quietly once as he died.

The second rebel, standing in the shadows between two huts, snapped a shot at Burns. The bullet missed, slamming into the stone wall and then sailing off with a whine that reverberated through the stillness of the evening. Burns leaped back around the corner and waited for a moment. There was no second shot and Burns got to one knee to peek around the corner. The rebel fired at him, the muzzle flash showing Burns where he hid.

Grinning to himself, Burns reached down and took a grenade from his belt. He leaned the dead man's rifle against the wall out of the way, pulled the pin of the grenade and waited for an instant. He let the spoon fly, counted to himself, and then threw the grenade like it was a baseball at the wall of the hut where the rebel hid. It hit the stone, bounced, and then exploded in a fountain of sparks and a spray of shrapnel. There was a shriek of pain from the shadows as the terrorist hiding there died, the explosion and shrapnel ripping him apart.

With that man dead, Burns ran from cover, dodged across the ground until he was near the hostage hut. He leaped to cover, dived under a bush, looked, and jumped to his feet, sprinting forward.

Inside the hut, Maude Wynter, alerted by the shooting and the explosion, had taken a position near the window, her back to the wall and facing the interior of the room. She turned her head so that she could see out without exposing herself to enemy fire. She watched Jihar lead a group of rebels from the mess hall. He pointed twice and the groups splintered, taking up firing positions and running toward the front gate.

She turned so she could see Bauman, her face a mask of anger and hatred. "It's that bloody Marine," she cried. Then she saw Halloran sitting in the chair, unable to move, unable to protect himself. She drew her pistol and stepped forward quickly, closer to Halloran, and aimed it at the center of his face.

Smiling, she pulled back the hammer with her thumb.

Bauman didn't hesitate. She threw the scalding tea at Wynter, catching her in the face. Wynter screamed, raising her hands to her face to scrub at the pain. Bauman kicked upward, hit Wynter on the wrist, sent the pistol sailing across the room, where it disappeared from sight.

Bauman rushed Wynter, but Wynter was ready now. She clasped her hands together and chopped downward, aiming at Bauman's neck. Bauman was momentarily stunned and staggered back away from the other woman.

Then Wynter grabbed a fork from the table and held it up, the tines pointed at Bauman. She stepped forward, pivoted slightly, and tried to stab Bauman in the eye, but the woman caught Wynter by the wrist. She stepped in, clipped Wynter with her hip to throw her off balance, and then yanked her around, tossing her at the wall. Wynter hit it with her back and dropped the fork as she was momentarily stunned by the pain in her lungs and through her stomach.

As Bauman scrambled for the pistol, Wynter screamed, her voice breaking, and leaped to Bauman's back, driving her to the floor. Bauman tried to turn, and landed on her back, Wynter above her. She grabbed Wynter's wrists as Wynter leaned down and tried to bite her throat, trying to rip out her jugular with bare teeth.

Bauman levered her arm free, let go of Wynter's wrist, and slammed her forearm into Wynter's face. Wynter rolled off Bauman, getting to her hands and knees. Bauman scrambled around, and Wynter dived for the pistol on the floor. Bauman kicked at Wynter, hitting her in the stomach, but the woman didn't stop.

At that moment, Burns crashed through the door. Wynter saw him. She forgot about the weapon and scrambled to the other door, throwing the table there out of the way. Beyond it was a circular staircase leading up away from the Marine.

Burns shot a glance at Bauman, who had retrieved the pistol and seemed to be all right. Halloran, still bound to the chair, seemed to be no worse for the wear and in no danger of dying soon. Burns ignored them both as he ran across the room. He stopped at the door, leaned his rifle against the wall and pulled his .45 from its holster.

He looked around the corner, but the spiral stairs were empty. He could hear no one on them and the light from the setting sun did little for him. He dived through the doorway, but wasn't fired on. He got to his feet and began climbing the stairs, working his way up slowly, carefully, his back to the center column, watching the steps and the walls for shadows that would indicate an ambush.

Finally he reached the top and saw a door that opened onto a parapet that ran around the outside of a minaret. Below him he could see men running around, but none of them seemed to have any idea what was happening. There were random shots directed at shadows, tracers flashing through the dusk, and the flickering of a couple of fires.

As Burns moved around the parapet, Wynter hurled herself at him, a knife clutched in her hand. She chopped downward with it, driving it through his equipment harness and into his shoulder. Grabbing her, he leaned into her and lifted her to his shoulders as she was about to strike again. With little effort he threw her out, off the roof, away from the parapet: "Die, *bitch!*"

Wynter screamed as she fell. She crashed into the ground, landing almost head first, caving in her skull, dying instantly. Burns stood there for a moment, his hands resting on the metal railing around the parapet, and then turned to rush back downstairs.

As he stepped into the room he saw Bauman crouched behind Halloran, her fingers working at the ropes that bound him. He was rocking in the chair, jerking at his hands, tugging, trying to help but only making it worse.

"Goddammit, woman," he shouted. "I didn't live this long to die tied to a chair! Cut me loose, for Chrissakes!"

As Burns moved to the chair, Bauman stood and stepped back. Burns drew his combat knife, a Marine-issue Kabar, and sliced through the ropes. Just at that moment, one of the rebels burst through the door and saw Bauman standing near the window. Without waiting, Burns snapped his knife at the man, the blade catching the rebel in the neck, driving through it. Blood washed down his chest and sides and as he fell, his eyes rolled up into his head.

Bauman spun then and fired twice, both rounds hitting the man, who was dead before he touched the floor.

In the main camp, the rebels were continuing to pour from the mess hall, from their barracks, from a communal room, and even from a couple of guard posts, running in all directions, firing from cover and from other buildings. Most hadn't found targets and were shooting at the shifting shadows caused by the setting sun and the light breeze.

* * *

On the roof of the monastery at one edge of the terrorist camp, James and Ruggieri tried to create a cross fire. They had used the Huey to fly them into position, and during the confusion of the brief fire-fight between Burns and a couple of the rebels, they had rappeled from the hovering helicopter to the flat roof. As soon as they had touched down, the ropes were cut loose and the helicopter pivoted, climbing away before the terrorists had a chance to fire at it.

James peeked over the edge of the roof, saw a huge rebel running across an open field, and started shooting at him, The bullets kicked up dirt around him, smashed into a wall behind him as he ran past it, but didn't hit him. James crawled across the roof-top to get into a better position, fired again, and missed the big man as he ducked into a building.

At the same time, a couple of rebels spotted him and began pouring fire up at him. James dropped flat on the rooftop, hugging it, trying to force his face deeper into it so that he could disappear. The smell of hot tar and old dirt filled his nostrils as he breathed rapidly. He was suddenly covered with sweat stinging his eyes and trickling down his sides and back. He was almost afraid to move as the terrorist bullets slammed into the building.

James tried to roll to his left, but the rebels had him spotted and began shooting rapidly, the tracers from their weapons lacing the darkening sky, bouncing high. When James dropped down again, they continued to shoot, not giving him a chance to move or return their fire.

Twenty feet away, Ruggieri, crouched in the shadows on the roof and protected by a short wall, glanced at James and saw what was happening. He saw the tracers ripping into the structure near James and then located the muzzle flashes of the enemy weapons. Ruggieri reached down and pulled a grenade from his belt. He jerked the pin free and dropped it to the roof, then, easing up slightly so that he could see better, he watched one of the rebels fire several shots at James. As the man ducked, Ruggieri threw his grenade, arcing it toward the two terrorists below him on another roof.

A second later there was an explosion, a showering of sparks and a rain of shrapnel as the grenade detonated. One of the rebels was thrown from his position to land sprawled a few feet from where he had been. The other, badly wounded, staggered into the open and then toppled over the side, falling to the ground below.

Cautiously James lifted his head and peeked down. He could see one man lying dead on the roof. There was no one shooting at him and he shot a glance over to Ruggieri, who was smiling at him.

"Hey, Ruge!" shouted James as he rolled to his side and pulled a candy bar from his pocket. It was a soft, deformed thing but a candy bar nonetheless. He flipped it across the roof at Ruggieri who caught it in his left hand. Ruggieri gave him a thumbs-up and a smile as he stuffed the candy into one of his own pockets.

They both then began to crawl across the roof in opposite directions so that they could command a large portion of the courtyard from their rooftop position. Neither fired indiscriminately, taking only good targets, dropping the enemy with short bursts from their automatic weapons. Ruggieri tossed grenades while James covered him.

* * *

At that same moment, Elias smashed through the wooden gate in his produce truck. Three rebels who had been on guard began firing into the side of the vehicle, trying to stop it and kill the occupants. The Israelis in the back opened fire with .30 caliber machine guns, their rapid chattering raking the yard around them.

There were a couple of fires burning, and in the flickering light, they could see men scrambling for cover. Each of the men with the machine guns sought targets, swinging their weapons to bear. They cut down the terrorists, chopping their feet out from under them, tumbling them into the dirt, and riddling the bodies. Their copper-jacketed bullets smashed into the chests of the fleeing rebels, slamming them to the ground. All around them, the terrorists were dying as Elias guided the truck to the center of the camp.

Burns had run from the hostage hut and was working his way from building to building, dodging bullets, and firing at the terrorists he saw. He watched the truck crash through the gate, backing into the center of the courtyard, the Israelis in the back firing into the enemy positions. Their tracers bounced into the terrorists' defensive positions or ricocheted high. He saw a couple of the rebels tumble into the dirt as the Israelis raked their hiding places.

From the right he saw a rebel break cover, running hunched over toward the driver's door of the produce truck. The man had his head down, as if he didn't want to see where he was going, but his destination was clear enough. Burns stepped around the corner of the hut, a dead terrorist's Uzi locked against his hip. He squeezed the trigger in a sustained burst and watched the bullets smash the terrorist to the ground, tumbling him as the rounds killed him, his weapon flying from his hands as he died and his blood began pooling under his body.

From the cab of the truck, Elias glanced at the dead body near his wheels. He grinned at Burns and continued to back toward the mess hall, where he knew that a dozen or more of the terrorists had taken refuge.

In the mess hall, Gavril saw the truck coming and opened fire, but his bullets seemed ineffective. The truck wouldn't stop, as relentless as the waves of the ocean. Finally, he gave up, backed away from the door, and then spun, running to the rear exit of the mess hall. He ran from the building, ducked down, and dodged across the compound, running from the shooting. He saw Jihar at the door to the weapons storeroom, but didn't stop there.

Jihar grabbed at the padlock and jerked on it. The key was locked in his desk across the compound, and there was no way for him to retrieve it. He stepped back and kicked, his foot connecting near the lock. The door vibrated with the impact and dirt cascaded downward. He kicked again and the wood splintered. The door flew inward, slamming into the wall, and as Jihar dived through, a half dozen bullets crashed into the wall and doorframe where he had been standing.

In front of him was a crate marked USMC and M47 DRAGON GUIDED MISSILE SYSTEM. He leaped across the room and began digging through the equipment stacked there, throwing it out of his way. He found a crowbar, and pried the lid from the dragon crate. The wood popped and splintered and the nails howled in protest. Jihar reached with his left hand, and pulled the wood free, tossing it out of his way. He dropped the crowbar to the floor and reached into the crate.

Across the courtyard, a hundred meters away, Halloran was firing from a window. There was a single rebel running toward the door of the hut. Halloran fired, missed, fired again, and then a third time. The rebel lost his balance and fell, rolling over and then lying motionless. Halloran put another bullet into the body to make sure. Then he glanced at the pistol as if he couldn't believe that it actually fired, or that when it had fired he had actually missed.

"Son of a bitch," he said.

He glanced out the window and then moved to the door. He ducked out of it, jammed his pistol into his pocket, and snatched up one of the submachine guns lying next to a dead terrorist. He crouched there for a moment, studying the landscape around him. There was a burst from the right and Halloran spun, rolling, and fired. He stitched the rebel from shoulder to hip, the bullets driving him back into the shadows where he collapsed. Halloran got to his feet, grabbed a second weapon, and leaped back into the hut.

Bauman was at one of the windows, Wynter's Walther in her hand, firing at the men who were running from building to building.

Halloran called to Bauman and flipped one of the machine guns to her. He then took up his position at one of the windows, searching for a target.

* * *

In the weapons room, Jihar stood in the doorway and saw Halloran reappear at the window. He hoisted the dragon to his shoulder and sighted on the hostage hut. Through the tracker scope he aligned the cross hairs on the window where Halloran stood. He armed the system and grinned to himself as he prepared to fire.

At that moment, Burns rounded the corner, saw Jihar, and dived at him, knocking him deeper into the hut to crash into the wooden crate. Burns leaped to follow, both men facing one another, their eyes locked as they each waited for the other to move. For a moment they stood like that, and then Burns attacked, feinted a front kick, and pirouetted to a reverse back kick, which was blocked. Burns turned to the left, stepping closer with a follow-up chop to Jihar's ear. The big man reeled back, a hand to his head as blood flowed through his fingers.

But then Jihar attacked, chopping at Burns, who blocked the blows, fighting back with a series of his own, only to have them stopped, too. Jihar kicked, but missed Burns. His foot smashed into the side of a crate, splintering the wood. Dancing to the right, he threw a punch at Burns, who ducked under it, coming up with a punch of his own that glanced off Jihar's side. Jihar kicked again and Burns blocked it by crossing his forearms to catch the foot. He tried to grab it to flip the terrorist, but lost his grip.

Jihar came at him then, punching. Burns staggered back under the weight of the attack, blocking the kicks and punches, absorbing the blows with his shoulders and hips. He tried to get enough distance between himself and Jihar to launch his own attack, but the big man kept coming, kept pressing him. Finally he caught Burns in the face with a massive right hand. Burns stumbled back, turning under the force of the blow, hitting the wall face first, but still on his feet. His vision had drawn down to a narrow tunnel surrounded by black so that he could only see things directly in front of him and all of them looked as if they were a long way off.

Jihar didn't hesitate. He was on Burns, slamming his big fists into Burns's back and kidneys, pounding him. Burns sagged against the wall, his face scraping against the rough surface, leaving bits of skin and lines of blood. He knew he had to act or die. He pivoted quickly, leading with his elbow, aiming low, expecting Jihar to duck. He caught the terrorist in the throat.

Jihar gasped, both in surprise and pain, and staggered back away from Burns. Now it was Burns who was in command. He moved in on the rebel, kicking and punching, landing blows to his enemy's head, chest and stomach. He kept hitting him, the blood flowing from Jihar's nose, mouth, and ears. Jihar was weaving but refused to go down.

Burns attacked with a vicious kick, but Jihar grabbed his foot, lifted, and twisted. Burns, caught off balance, crashed to the floor on his back, crushing a small box sitting there. Burns tried to roll to the side but Jihar moved in, kicking at Burns's unprotected side. He hit Burns on the jaw, flipping him to his back. Burns was stunned by the blow and his vision began to fade.

Jihar reached down and hauled Burns to his feet as if he weighed nothing. Reveling in his own brute strength, he slammed Burns against a large wooden crate, which collapsed. Weakly, Burns tried to get up, but Jihar just grabbed him in a crushing bear hug. He slammed Burns into a wall with enough force to nearly rock the building. Then he began to squeeze, slowly mashing the breath from Burns.

Burns struggled to free an arm. He could feel his ribs giving under the power. Jihar increased the pressure, his face buried against Burns's chest, a growl escaping from his lips, his only thought to kill this Marine as he had killed the other one.

But Burns wasn't through. He levered a hand up behind Jihar and grabbed a handful of hair, pulling. Jihar's head came up slowly, but not enough for Burns to free himself. He continued to pull, increasing the pressure until he felt Jihar shift just a little more. Suddenly, Burns snapped a hand free and hit Jihar in the jaw with a short jab that had almost no power behind it. He pressed his hand to Jihar's chin, forcing his head back, but the big man just squeezed harder, hoping to kill Burns in seconds. Burns's hand slipped free and Jihar buried his face again so that Burns couldn't get at it. Instead, Burns jammed his thumb into Jihar's eye.

Jihar bellowed in pain and rage and tried to slam Burns into the wall, but Burns kept digging at the eye, gouging at it, reaming the socket. Jihar was screaming as Burns popped the eyeball free, the bloodied pulp dangling at the end of the optic nerve.

Suddenly, Jihar dropped Burns, and grabbed at his blood-covered face. He was no longer aware of what was happening around him. He had lost track of everything. He could not think. He could only feel the white-hot pain in his eye, washing everything else from his mind.

Burns grabbed him and spun him so that his back was against the rough wall. Burns levered his forearm up under the terrorist's chin, holding him pinned there as the man screamed incoherently. Burns rammed the heel of his hand up under the man's nose, smashing it in a splash of blood, splintering the soft bone and cartilage, and driving it into Jihar's brain. Burns released Jihar, who collapsed to the floor, landing on his back, blood pouring from his nose to cover his chin and shoulders, dead.

Burns dropped to his knees, his head down, breathing hard. Slowly the curtain of black receded and he could see everything around him. Carefully, he got to his feet and staggered across the floor. There was a shotgun lying there and Burns picked it up, racked it once to make sure that a round was chambered, and then picked up the ejected shell. He pushed it into the bottom of the weapon and stumbled to the door. He hesitated there for a moment.

Across the way, he could see the produce truck used by the Israelis to penetrate the terrorists' camp. In the back were two commandos who had given up using their machine guns and were now hosing down the enemy with flamethrowers. They were spraying everything with liquid fire, turning the mess hall into a sea of flame that forced the rebels hiding in there to flee. The tongues of flame set a car on fire, a palm tree, anything they could reach. They lighted the compound brightly, making the terrorists visible as they tried to run from their hiding places. Another commando opened fire with a machine gun, cutting down the enemy who weren't covered with flame. There was very little return fire from anywhere.

At the side of the truck, using it for cover, Ruggieri and James were pouring a stream of bullets into a building, shattering the windows and splintering the window frames. There were a few halfhearted return shots that weren't well aimed, and then nothing.

Then, near the truck, Burns saw Elias kneeling on the ground, a half dozen Israeli commandos surrounding him. He pointed and three of them sprinted toward a short, squat building. Two of them took positions on either side of the door, while the third riddled the knob and lock with a burst from his Uzi. He kicked it open and tossed a grenade into the black interior as he dived to one side. When it detonated, blowing out the remaining glass in the windows, he dived through the door. There was a wild burst of firing and then silence. The commando emerged a moment later carrying an AK-47 in each hand and another slung over his back. He had jammed a couple of magazines into his pockets.

Halloran and Bauman ran from the hostage hut then, angling toward the truck. Halloran fired a burst from his hip as he ran, the bullets slamming into another small hut, but there was no return fire from it. They joined forces with the commandos, letting Elias lead them.

As Burns ran from the weapons hut, he saw Amin, the Minister of Finance, and Mustafa, his driver, trying to get to the car. Neither of them had seen him as they ran. Burns angled toward them. As he approached, Mustafa reached up under the short jacket he wore, trying to draw his weapon. Burns didn't hesitate. He fired once with his shotgun, the round catching Mustafa high in the chest, blasting him off his feet. He landed against the side of the car and slipped to the ground, leaving a streak of bright blood that was barely visible against the dark paint.

Amin slid to a stop and stared in horror at his dead driver: the waxy look on his face; the wide open eyes that were just whites giving him a strange, blank expression; the blood that soaked his clothes. Slowly

Amin turned so that he could see Burns. He stood crouched, his hands wide open, his fingers splayed.

Burns said nothing to the man. His eyes shifted to the dead terrorist on the ground and then back to Amin.

"I'm Amin. The Minister of Finance," he said, the terror in his voice turning it cold.

Burns continued to stare as if waiting for Amin to explain it all to him.

"I'm Amin," he said again, his voice pleading, as if begging for his life. "The Minister of—"

Burns aimed his weapon and pulled the trigger. The blast hit Amin in the stomach, blowing him off his feet so that he landed on his butt and tumbled. He wrapped his arms around his midsection, moaned, and then rolled to his back. Burns racked the shotgun, ejecting the spent shell, keeping the barrel pointing at Amin, waiting for him to move, and said, "You ain't shit."

Around him the firing tapered off until it was only an occasional *pop* from a rifle and a quick, short burst from a submachine gun. He could hear the fires burning around him and saw shadows dancing among them. The Israelis were moving through the camp, clearing the buildings, but it looked as if the raid was over. The terrorists were dead, their bodies littering the ground among the burning buildings and ruined vehicles. Burns shrugged at the dead Minister of Finance and began to walk across the compound toward the others.

CHAPTER TWELVE

Nearly the entire rebel camp was in flames. Fires had been started by the tracers and by the flamethrowers and grenades. Some of the huts and buildings had been damaged by grenades and others had been destroyed by Elias and his truck. Bodies lay scattered on the ground, their weapons near their outstretched hands. The Israelis had picked up some of the equipment and were sweeping through, collecting the rest of it. The fires threw a flickering light on the camp as the smoke billowed from the flames, obscuring the sky.

There was sporadic gunfire as the commandos and the Marines tried to clear the buildings using the method learned by the armies of World War II. One man would blow open a door, shoot the lock off and kick it in, or just riddle it with machine-gun fire until he could toss a grenade in. After the explosion, two men would dive through the door, one going left and the other right. They would come up firing at anything that moved in the building. Once the ground floor was cleared that way, they would work their way up the stairs and clear each of the rooms on the second floor.

Off to the right, one of the flamethrower teams

was working to clear the buildings there, but instead of using grenades, they opened the door with the flamethrower. When the door had burned away, the man would slowly advance, sweeping the flames from one side to the other until the entire room was engulfed in fire and the occupants either dead or cut down by the riflemen as they tried to flee.

As the shooting died away and the explosions of the grenades stopped punctuating the night, Halloran moved out of the hostage hut. He was flattened against the exterior wall of the building, an Uzi held in both hands. He swiveled his head from right to left, checking the field around him. He could see a couple of terrorists sprawled in the dirt facedown. Then he saw Burns run from the weapons storeroom. Burns slid to a halt near one of the bodies, jerked the Uzi from the dead fingers, searched the rebel for ammunition, and slammed a fresh magazine into the weapon. He looked up, made sure that there was a round chambered and then ran off toward the front of the camp.

Halloran watched the younger man for a moment, glad that Burns had survived the assault. He breathed deeply, as if he couldn't get enough air, and then ran off, joining the others who were cleaning the camp of the few surviving terrorists.

He ran by the truck. Bauman sat in the cab, pumping the gas pedal, and twisting the key, trying to get the engine started. Behind it Ruggieri and James were helping the Israelis, including Elias, load the wounded in the back to transport them from the scene. He stopped for a moment, nodded at the two Marines, and then left them.

As one of the commandos slammed the doors, latching them, a grenade arced out of the night. It landed in the middle of the group and before any of them could react, it exploded, spraying hot shrapnel around them, riddling the doors of the truck and the people standing near them. Everyone fell, some of them wounded, others dying, and a couple of them dead.

At the sound of the detonation, Burns halted and spun. He saw Halloran close to him. Both men watched as Bauman leaped from the cab of the truck and raced around it. She dropped to her knees as she saw the bodies lying behind it. She crawled to her brother, who was lying motionless among the bodies of his men and the Marines. There was a quiet moaning from one of the Israelis. James struggled to sit up, his eyes on the body of Ruggieri, who had lost most of one arm when the grenade went off.

Burns and Halloran sprinted to the truck. As they reached it, a Land Rover flew through the front gate, its wheels throwing rocks and kicking up clouds of dust. Burns fired a short burst at it, but the Land Rover was already out of range, rocketing down the road.

Bauman was clinging to the lifeless body of her brother, his face streaked with dirt and smeared with blood that was beginning to stain her clothes. Burns crouched next to her and took her shoulders in his hands, turning her, knowing what she was thinking: that it was unfair, because they had won the fight; unfair, because it was over, with the majority of the terrorists dead and the rest fleeing for safety in the mountains and desert around them; that they shouldn't have taken any more casualties because there was no resistance left in the camp.

As their eyes met, she grasped at him, as if she

could take strength from him, and then cried out, "Gavril! It was Gavril!"

Burns released her and she fell back, her face on her brother. She was crying uncontrollably, embracing him, mumbling that he couldn't be dead. Burns got to his feet, glanced at her shaking shoulders, and then turned to look at the mountain road leading from the camp. There was a spreading cloud of dust along it and in the distance was the sound of the Land Rover's racing engine. Burns spun and ran for a jeep parked near one of the huts, the body of a terrorist slumped in the seat. Burns grabbed the shoulder of the man and threw the body to the ground, stepping over it.

He turned the ignition switch, heard the engine rumble to life, and rammed it into gear with a loud grinding. He jammed his foot to the floorboards, spun the wheel, and roared off. He slammed on the brakes and slid to a stop next to the weapons room in a cloud of dust. He leaped from the jeep, ran inside, and grabbed the dragon that Jihar had been going to fire. He tossed it in the back of the jeep and looked up toward Halloran, who was working on the wounded James. Halloran looked at him then, and held up a blood-covered hand, thumb in the air, telling Burns to get the fucking son of a bitch.

Burns climbed in, slammed the jeep into gear, and roared off, the rear tires spinning wildly, throwing up a huge cloud of dust and dirt. He whipped the wheel around, aimed at the gate, and flew through it. He slowed long enough to see the fading plume of dust from Gavril's vehicle below him on the road that led back to the city. Burns didn't hesitate. He turned to the right, used the road for a moment, and then left it, almost driving over a cliff. The mountain side was steep, nearly a seventy-degree angle, but Burns didn't care. He started down, his foot on the gas, adding to his momentum. He bounced over a couple of large rocks, dodged a boulder, and felt the bottom drop out as he crashed into a ravine. The jeep climbed the other side as Burns dropped it into low and gave it gas. It was suddenly as if he were in free-fall, dropping down the side of a cliff rather than trying to drive down the steep slope of a mountain.

Far in front of him and far below him, he could see the Land Rover, a black mark on the leading edge of the dust cloud. Burns slipped into second gear and tried to pick up speed, the dust flying behind him. He smashed through a large bush, crushing it under his wheels, bounced high over a log, and hit a flat stretch. The jarring and the bouncing were shaking him badly, making it hard to breathe. There were sharp pains in his back each time the jeep bottomed out, and his shoulder felt as if it were on fire. He tried to keep his teeth clamped tight so that he didn't bite off his own tongue, but he didn't let up. To catch Gavril, he couldn't.

He turned again, changing the angle so that he looked like a linebacker about to nail the wide receiver, getting ready to come out on the road ahead of Gavril. He dropped back into first gear, the right wheels bounding over a boulder that threatened to tip the jeep. Burns leaned into it, shifting his weight so that the jeep fell back to all four wheels and continued the kamikaze descent.

He was closer to the Land Rover and the road. He could see the shape of the driver behind the wheel. Burns turned, charged up a shallow ravine, whipped to the right, out of it, and continued his madman's descent. He could see that Gavril was scared, pushing his Land Rover to the limit, taking corners too fast, but getting away with it.

Burns entered another ravine. The front wheels bounced over a log, bottomed out, and then left the ground again. He floored, the rear wheels spinning, digging deeper, but couldn't get any traction. He jumped from the jeep, grabbed the dragon, and ran up the side of the ravine toward the road.

Gavril looked back, but could no longer see the jeep chasing him. He could no longer see the cloud of dust behind it and assumed that whoever had been chasing him had crashed. He slowed slightly, breathing easier. He wiped the sweat from his face with the sleeve of his jacket. He rubbed his chin with the back of his hand and rocked back in his seat, feeling good because he had gotten away.

He rounded a corner and slammed on the brakes, locking the wheels. The Land Rover fishtailed, slid sideways, throwing up a cloud of dirt, momentarily obscuring the road and everything in it. Gavril felt fear for the first time in a decade. He felt his stomach flutter and the skin at the back of his neck crawl, making him tingle. As soon as the Land Rover stopped, Gavril clawed at the door handle trying to get out, his eyes locked forward.

Burns stood there, the dragon on his shoulder—a long, thick, bazookalike object with a fat optical sight stuck near the front of it, and a large protrusion on the back. The tripod attached to the front dangled two or three feet from the ground. Burns was staring through the optical sight, watching Gavril, grinning at him, letting him think that he was going to get clear. As the door was thrown open, Burns pulled the trigger so that the missile was launched, the rocket igniting as it was ejected from the tube.

Gavril saw the missile fired as if in slow motion and knew that he could do nothing about it. He screamed, his voice lost in the sound of the missile as the rockets ignited and flew at him, trailing the guidance wires.

A split second later the missile hit the Land Rover and exploded, lifting the vehicle from its wheels and tossing it into the air like a toy. Flame shot up and the gas tank detonated, throwing burning debris into the road and all over the shoulder. Chunks of metal rained down, hitting the ground with sharp metallic rings.

Burns stood watching for a moment, staring into the burning Land Rover, looking for some sign that Gavril had survived, waiting for him to reappear, but there was no movement. Burns threw the dragon into the bushes at the side of the road, grunting with the effort. It hit and bounced, rolling into a ravine. He stared at it for a moment and then wondered about the action. He wondered what had prompted it. The dragon wasn't responsible for the deaths in the camp, or the destruction of the Land Rover. It was a tool. One that he had used effectively and one that hadn't let him down. He regretted the action, but didn't go after it. Instead, he turned and walked back up to where he had left his jeep.

It was jammed on a log but he could see that it would be easy to free. He rolled a rock so that it was leaning against the front of the rear wheel. He climbed in and started the engine. He shifted it into four-wheel drive and touched the gas pedal, feeling the jeep inch forward until the rear wheel was against the rock. Then he punched it, heard the engine race, and bounced over the rock and the log. He stopped then, looking back at the burning wreck in the middle of the road. He drove up to it, spun the wheel, and guided the jeep around the Land Rover. He stopped close enough to feel the heat from the flames and looked into where the front seat should have been. He tried to see Gavril's body but there was nothing in it that looked even vaguely human. He wanted to see it to prove to himself that Gavril was dead, but knew that it was only something he felt he had to do. There was no way for Gavril to have survived the explosion of the missile.

Finally he shifted into gear and headed toward the camp. As he approached, he could see the fire and smoke. At the gate he stopped and could see another jeep parked nearby. Burns got out and saw that it held the body of Ruggieri. James sat next to it, a large white bandage stained red wrapped around his arm. Halloran sat in the front, his damaged hand cradled in the crook of his other arm. He was staring to the front, looking out over the desert.

Behind them, in the compound, a dozen fires still burned, bodies scattered everywhere, but there were no longer any weapons or equipment near them. Somebody had gone through the camp taking everything that would have been useful to any other terrorists. Burns glanced at the weapons room and saw that it was burning fiercely, as if someone had torched it because they couldn't carry everything away.

The produce truck hadn't been moved. There were no longer any bodies around it. They had all been picked up and either put in the back to be transported into the capital city, or carried to the jeep. The single exception was a body covered with a sheet. Elli Bauman was crouched near it, holding one of the hands. She stood and stepped back as two of the Israeli commandos picked it up and carefully loaded it into the back of the produce truck. As they shut the doors, she moved forward and leaned her head against the rear and began to cry again, harder. Her hands were clenched at her sides.

Burns moved toward her and gently touched her shoulder. When she didn't respond, he turned her so that she faced him. She looked up into his eyes, felt her own fill again and spill over. She scrubbed at her eyes angrily, as if embarrassed that she was crying.

"When are they going to stop killing us?" she asked him quietly.

Burns pulled her close, holding her tightly. He hesitated for a moment and then said, "Remember, it was your people who said, 'Never again.' We'll never give up."

For an instant longer he held her and then broke away, unable to think of anything else to say. What could he say? That the sacrifice was worthwhile? That they had broken the back of a terrorist group that had been responsible for a hundred deaths in the last few days and weeks? That they had destroyed a group of men and women who were terrorists preying on the weak? Did that somehow make the death of her brother any less traumatic? Any less tragic? There were just no words that helped at a time like this. She would have to come to grips with it all herself, work through it by herself, until she had an answer that worked for her.

He left her there and started toward the jeep, where Halloran and James waited. Halfway there he stopped and turned to look back. Elli had turned away from him and slowly walked to the cab of the truck. She climbed in and slammed the door. Looking neither left nor right, she leaned her head against the window and waited for the driver to take her out of the terrorist camp. The engine started and the truck pulled away from him, moving in the opposite direction.

Burns watched it for a moment and then started toward the jeep. He saw James reach inside his shirt and pull out the tiny flag that Ramirez's mother had made for him. James shifted around and grabbed the whip antenna on the back of the jeep, pulling it down toward him. He tried to fasten it to the antenna but had only limited luck. He stripped some adhesive from his bandage, worked at it again and succeeded. He released the antenna, letting it spring upright.

Burns walked closer to the jeep and looked up at the flag. Somehow that answered the question. Somehow that made the sacrifice worthwhile. Maybe Elli Bauman wouldn't be able to understand that right away, but someday she would. Someday she would know that individual sacrifices were worthwhile when they helped preserve freedom for the whole group. Elias and Ruggieri and all the others had died to make sure that the majority could live without fear. That day might still be in the future, but it was a day that was coming, and the sacrifice made that night was one of the reasons.

Keeping his eye on the flag, Burns climbed into the jeep. He turned and saw Halloran nod as if approving of the whole mission. Burns started the engine, dropped the jeep into gear, popped the clutch, and they leaped forward.

CHANCE

The Maverick with the Winning Hand

A blazing new series of Western excitement featuring a high-rolling rogue with a thirst for action!

by Clay Tanner

CHANCE   75160-7/$2.50US/$3.50Can
Introducing Chance—a cool-headed, hot-blooded winner—who knows what he wants and how to get it!

CHANCE #2   75161-5/$2.50US/$3.50Can
Riverboat Rampage
From ghostly spirits on the river to a Cajun beauty who's ready and willing to stoke up big trouble, Chance is the man women love and varmints love to hate!

and coming soon

CHANCE #3   75162-3/$2.50US/$3.50Can
Dead Man's Hand
Framed for murder, the gambling man breaks out of jail and in a fast shuffle heads upriver to settle the score.

CHANCE #4   75163-1/$2.50US/$3.50Can

KILLSQUAD

by Frank Garrett

WANTED: A world strike force—the last hope of the free world—the ultimate solution to global terrorism!

THE WEAPON: Six desperate and deadly inmates from Death Row led by the invincible Hangman...

THE MISSION: To brutally destroy the terrorist spectre wherever and whenever it may appear...

WORLD WAR II
Edwin P. Hoyt